LIVING
DANGEROUSLY

LIVING
DANGEROUSLY

DAN LATUS

ROBERT HALE · LONDON

Robert Hale Limited
Clerkenwell House
Clerkenwell Green
London EC1R 0HT

www.halebooks.com

Typeset in New Century Schoolbook
Printed in Great Britain by Berforts Information Press Ltd

Chapter One

JIMMY MACK, MY neighbour, said, 'It looks like snow tonight.'

I looked at the sky, recalled the forecast I'd heard a few hours earlier and shook my head. 'I don't think so, Jim,' I said confidently.

It snowed that night. It snowed heavily. In the morning the white stuff was two-feet deep across the North York Moors, and the drifts were deeper still. Whitby was cut off once again. I wasn't worried about any of that, but I was troubled by the footprints all around my cottage. There was no easy explanation for them, and given what I do for a living there's always people trying to get even, and looking to do me harm.

Someone, some solitary person, had made two or three circuits of the cottage and then trudged back along the track to the point where it joined the road. A vehicle had been waiting there, a heavy-duty machine. Probably a big four-by-four, judging by the tyre tread pattern. Maybe a pickup truck.

The footprints were small. Possibly a very small man's, but I thought they were more likely to have been made by a woman. It could have been a youngster, but because of the vehicle I was inclined to rule out a child.

That was as much as I could tell. Having completed my early-morning inspection, I kicked the snow off my boots and went back inside to get some breakfast.

*

What could I say? Not much. Someone – possibly a woman – had walked round my home two or three times during the night. The footprints, the deep holes, had not been even partially filled in by new snow. So whoever it was had arrived after the snow stopped falling, which would have been sometime after three. That was when the rustling and whispering against my bedroom window had ceased.

And they had come before first light, a little before seven. I had been awake since then and would have heard a vehicle arriving or starting up again anywhere nearby.

So what had it been? A reconnaissance?

And who had it been, and what had they wanted?

I had no idea. Someone had left me a nice little mystery I didn't really need.

After breakfast I made my way over to see Jimmy Mack, a virtually retired fisherman who lives in the neighbouring cottage here at Risky Point. There's just the two of us on this isolated cliff top on the Cleveland coast. Our cottages used to be part of a hamlet peopled by ironstone miners and fishermen and their families, but coastal erosion has taken away all but Jimmy's place and mine. One day it will likely take ours, too, as we both know full well. We live dangerously at Risky Point, like a few other people on the Cleveland coast.

'So you were right about the snow, Jim.'

He gave me a pitying look, as if to say I was a fool for ever doubting him.

'I could feel it in my bones. I can always tell.'

He was on about his arthritis again, I supposed, which seemed to be an infallible guide to all sorts of impending meteorological events.

'You didn't hear anything unusual during the night, did you? A vehicle along the track, say, or someone mooching about?'

He shook his head and looked at me with heightened interest, weighing my question up. 'Come in,' he said, sensing a diverting story and opening the door wide.

I followed him inside and shut the door after me.

'Someone was about,' I said, flopping into a chair in front of the fire. 'There's footprints all around my place.'

'That right?' He settled himself in the chair on the other side of the hearth and said with a grin, 'Well, you're the private investigator.'

I just scowled at him.

So it was a mystery. And there was little more to be said. Jimmy didn't have the answer, and I wasn't going to start speculating in front of him. I didn't want him to start worrying.

'That's a nice bit of fire,' I said, holding out my hands to feel the heat from the blaze of driftwood in the stone hearth.

He nodded and said, 'I could do with collecting some more wood before winter sets in proper.'

'I'll give you a hand. I could do with some myself.'

I did wonder if he would still be able to get down the path to the beach. He wasn't so good any more even on the flat, and that path was something special. You could do with roping up before you tackled it in wet weather. But I kept that thought to myself. I would go alone if necessary – like I had the last time, and the one before that.

'I'm going to try to get into Redcar in a bit, Jim. Anything I can get for you? Or do you want to come with me, perhaps?'

'Come with you?' He shook his head. 'What in? Your old tin can? No thanks! Anyway, I've got everything I need right here.'

Typical. Gratitude in spades. I sighed and got to my feet.

'Old tin can indeed! That Land Rover was built for weather like this,' I told him sternly. 'It comes into its own on a day like today.'

'Ice-box on wheels,' he said with a chuckle.

He wasn't far wrong about that, but I wasn't going to admit it.

'This might be him now,' he said suddenly, fixing me with a concentrated stare.

'Who?'

'Your night visitor, coming back.'

I walked over to the window. A big silver vehicle was bumping gently along the track. There was nothing wrong with Jimmy's hearing, whatever his other ailments. I made for the door.

'Don't let him in,' Jimmy said with a chuckle. 'That's my advice. It's probably trouble. Tell him you're out.'

Two people got out of the car. A man and a woman. Potential clients, they looked like. No one else would have come visiting on a day like this.

They spotted me and stood waiting, standing a little apart; a well-dressed couple looking ill at ease about something. The man had his head up and was looking around with exaggerated interest, as if he had to have something to do. The woman seemed withdrawn, closed in on herself. Feeling the cold, perhaps. She had her head pulled down into her neck, and a big coat collar turned up over her ears.

'Can I help you?'

'Mr Doy?' the man asked, turning to me with a polite smile.

'That's me, yes. Frank Doy.'

'Can you spare us a few minutes of your time, Mr Doy? There's something we'd like to discuss with you.'

8

'Certainly. Come on inside. It's too cold to stand out here.'

They followed me indoors, first taking the trouble to knock the snow off their shoes – a gesture I appreciated.

'Nice and warm in here!' the man said cheerfully, rubbing his hands together. 'You can't beat a wood stove. I'm Josh Steele, by the way. And this is my wife, Anne.'

We shook hands, and I smiled and ushered them to chairs around the stove. Warm as it was, the woman was slow to pull her head out of her collar. Frozen, probably. Perhaps their in-car heater was no better than mine.

'Coffee?' I queried. 'Only instant, I'm afraid.'

'That would be great,' the husband said with fake enthusiasm.

I filled the kettle, switched it on and turned back to them.

'What were the roads like? Any trouble getting here?'

'Plenty of snow,' the husband said, 'but no trouble getting here. I've got off-road tyres on that vehicle – four hundred quid apiece. It will go anywhere, any conditions.'

I nodded and made the coffee, already fearing I wasn't going to like him very much. But he obviously had money, which was something in his favour. I wish all my clients had money.

'So what can I do for you?'

'Well,' he began cautiously, 'we have a little problem you may be able to help us with. At least, my wife thinks—'

'Oh, shut up, Josh!' the wife said briskly. 'We have a major problem, not a little one.'

I turned towards her, surprised. Potential clients don't usually disagree with each other in the first few seconds of speaking to me.

My surprise grew as she turned down her collar, unbuttoned her coat and shook a little snow out of her hair. I realized then that I knew her.

'Hello, Frank,' she said with a sad smile. 'Frank, we want you to help save our son. He's in terrible danger.'

Chapter Two

THE FOUR MEN in the parked pickup truck sat quietly, waiting, watching the snow come down. The truck was stolen but only in the past half hour, too recently for the theft to have been reported. So they had a little time on their side.

Eddie, in the front passenger seat, took out a cigarette packet.

'Put it away!' snapped Blue, the driver.

Eddie turned, ready to argue.

'Put it away.'

Sullenly, Eddie put the packet away. He remembered then that Blue had said DNA could be picked up off fag ends, which was a good reason for not smoking on the job. He knew that. It was just that he'd forgotten. The tension was getting to him.

'He's late,' he murmured.

Blue shook his head. 'Taking his time, that's all. Relax.'

Blue right again, Eddie thought reluctantly. You couldn't fault him.

Another three or four minutes of nothing happening followed. The street was dead. It was just industrial compounds and storage sheds and factory units. No houses or shops. No pubs. And at night, no people.

Plenty of light, though, Blue thought with a grimace. Enough security lights to illuminate an entire fucking city. The white stuff didn't help either. It was like being on stage.

He didn't say anything to the others but he knew they couldn't sit here with the engine running much longer. Some sort of patrol would be along sooner or later, cops or private security. But if they left now they would have to abandon the job, for tonight at least. Logan wouldn't like that. Blue smiled and shook his head. Logan. So what?

'I don't like the snow,' Eddie said with a shiver.

Blue didn't like it either, but he was thinking more of exposure and footprints than temperature.

'I can hear something,' Chas snapped from one of the back seats.

Blue wound the window down and stuck his head out. Then he heard it, too. A distant noisy engine, coming closer. He frowned. Something big, but it didn't sound like a wagon.

'It's not him,' he said over his shoulder. 'Relax, fellas.'

But it was. Half a minute later a double-decker bus careered round the corner fifty yards ahead. They knew it had to be Big Cyril driving even before it straightened up and came roaring at them without lights.

'Jesus Christ!' shouted Manny, the fourth man in the truck. 'What's he fucking doing?'

The bus raced towards them – at them! Blue instinctively braced himself for the collision. Then the squealing started as Big Cyril slammed on the brakes. The bus shuddered, swayed violently from side to side and finally stopped just a few feet away.

Blue shook his head, swore and threw his door open. Bloody Cyril! He heard a couple of the others laughing – with relief probably – but he wasn't amused.

Big Cyril was. He was grinning his head off when he jumped down to the road. Everything was a game to him.

'Where's the wagon?' Blue demanded.

11

'Couldn't get it started, boss. But I figured this would do just as well.'

Blue thought fast. The bus wasn't what he wanted but it would have to do.

'OK. Turn it round. Go in backwards, if you don't want a concrete post through your chest.'

Big Cyril got back in the cab, found reverse and manoeuvred the bus until it straddled the road, its back end pointing at the high security fence on the far side. He leant out of the window and looked at Blue. Blue nodded. Big Cyril engaged gear, revved the engine and sent the bus hurtling backwards at the fence.

The first collision didn't do the job. The wagon with the snow plough blade on the front would have gone straight through first go, and out the other side, but not this rickety, thin-shelled thing. Instead, the back end of the bus crumpled and a shower of glass flew through the air. Blue motioned to Big Cyril to pull out and try again.

On the fourth attempt the bus, now perceptibly shorter and probably an insurance write-off, went straight through the weakened fence and into the timber compound beyond. Blue waved the others forward. They ran into the compound with jerry cans snatched from the pickup and began sloshing petrol over the nearest stacks of timber.

When they were done, he waited until they were all back through the gap in the fence. Then he lit a primed rag and tossed it onto the end of a petrol trail, before turning to trot back to the truck to join the others.

They took off immediately, without waiting to see what happened. They drove at a steady, sensible speed back to where they had parked the car a couple of miles away. There they swapped vehicles, set the truck on fire, and sped off again, all in a matter of minutes, Blue driving.

He stopped the car on the other side of the river, from where they had a good view. They could see flames reaching into the night sky, headed by a towering column of sparks.

'Like bonfire night,' Eddie said with approval.

Blue grinned at him and said, 'You can have that cigarette now.'

Chapter Three

'ANNE FENWICK,' I murmured with a smile. 'As was, that is. It's been a long time.'

She nodded and gave me a wry smile back. 'It certainly has.'

We had known each other when we were young, moving with the same crowd, enjoying the same music. Then the world had moved on, and I couldn't tell you when I'd last seen her. Long before she got married anyway. I had forgotten about her, but it seemed as if she hadn't forgotten me. Why else would she have been here?

'So what's this about?' I asked.

Her husband took up the story.

'I'm a businessman, Frank. Various strings to my bow. Lots of industrial properties. For some time now we've been experiencing a wave of vandalism, and other attacks of one sort or another. Arson, break-ins, thefts ...' He shrugged. 'You know the sort of thing.'

I nodded. It was a common enough story, although much depended on what your business was and where it was located.

'You want me to look at your security?' I glanced from one to the other of them and added, 'I thought you said it was about your son?'

Anne grimaced and said, 'It is. The other stuff doesn't really matter.'

'I'm just giving him some background,' Josh said, sounding defensive. 'There's a vendetta against us. That's what it amounts to.'

'Are the police on it?' I asked.

'They are,' he admitted. 'Not that that's done any good.'

'And is this linked to your son?'

Josh nodded and took a sip of his coffee. I was ready to be apologetic about the coffee but I don't think he even noticed what he was drinking.

'Unfortunately, the lad got himself into a spot of bother.'

'For God's sake, Josh!' Anne snapped at him. 'He killed someone.'

'Well …'

'He killed someone,' she reiterated, staring hard at him, challenging him. 'Let's not beat about the bush.'

He shut up then, not surprisingly. She had winded him. I felt inclined to wince on his behalf.

'Tell me what happened,' I said in a gentle tone, anxious to defuse the increasingly tense atmosphere. 'Then I might be able to tell you if I can help.'

'It was a road accident,' Anne said. 'Tom was just turned seventeen. He hadn't been driving long, and he'd been drinking with his pals. On the way home, just over a year ago, he knocked another young boy over. The boy died.

'Tom was convicted of causing his death, drink-driving etcetera, but because of mitigating circumstances he was given only a year in youth custody.'

'And banned from driving,' Josh added.

Anne shrugged, impatient with the qualifying remark, and said, 'He's just been let out.'

I nodded, and wondered what the mitigating circumstances could have been. His youth, perhaps? Or a good lawyer, more likely. Even so, it was obviously a bad situation.

But the way Anne had told the story was good. No flannel at all. Just a straightforward, simple and unemotional recital of the facts. Josh wasn't up to that. He couldn't help himself trying to put a gloss on things to make the bare facts look better.

Now all I needed to do was find out what had really happened, and why they were worried about their son. After that, I might be able to tell them if it was a job for me, or for somebody more like a psychiatrist – or a marriage counsellor.

"What kind of car was Tom driving?"

'A BMW 7-series,' Anne said with an angry look at her husband.

'Whose was it?'

'His – Tom's.'

I blinked and looked at Josh for corroboration. He nodded. 'We gave him it for his birthday.'

I was astonished, having assumed it had been an old banger with faulty brakes and steering. They could have been the mitigating circumstances.

'*You* gave it him!' Anne snapped. 'I wanted him to have a little Renault Clio, or something sensible like that.'

'Big cars are safer,' Josh protested.

'Oh, yes!'

By now I was beginning to think of sending them both packing, and definitely with a referral to Relate.

'For his seventeenth birthday?' I queried, trying hard not to sound too aghast. 'A BMW 7-series? That's a big present.'

'I have a car dealership,' Josh said defiantly.

'You didn't even give him a second-hand one,' Anne said. 'Oh, no! It had to be a brand new, top-of-the-range bloody Beamer!'

Wisely, Josh didn't say another word.

I wondered where we were going with this. So far, the only thing I'd heard that I might be able to help with was the security issue.

'Tell me more about the attacks on your business premises.'

'They're coordinated,' Josh said, 'and we know who's doing the coordinating.'

'Oh?'

'The lad's father – the lad that was knocked over.'

'And killed!' Anne pointed out again.

Josh didn't disagree.

'He's some sort of gangster,' Anne added wearily.

Ah! I was beginning to understand.

'That's why you said there was a vendetta?'

Josh said yes and Anne nodded. For once, something had been said to which they could both agree.

While we were on safe ground, I looked at Anne and asked, 'Were you here earlier? Earlier this morning, I mean?'

'Here?' she said, looking puzzled.

'At the cottage.'

'Of course not. I've never been here before in my life. You know that.'

So Jimmy had been wrong about my nocturnal visitor returning, and I was still left wondering who had made the footprints.

'Your boy, Tom, is out now, you said?'

'Three days ago,' Anne confirmed.

I was still waiting to hear what they wanted from me, and still wondering if they had come to the right person.

'So how can I help?'

Josh came in now, as if he'd been eagerly waiting in the wings for just that question. 'The other lad's father has threatened to kill Tom in reprisal.'

'As well as launching attacks on your business premises?'

He nodded. 'We want you to look after Tom for a bit. Keep him safe.'

I didn't ask the obvious question: *How the hell do you expect me to do that?* Instead, I remained patient and tried to be understanding.

'Go on,' I said.

'It was the wife's idea,' he said shortly.

I turned back to Anne.

'We want you to take him away somewhere, Frank, and keep him away until this thing is settled. Anywhere! We don't care where you go.'

'You can name your price,' Josh added. 'I've brought ten grand in cash with me for expenses, to get you started. And I'll give you a cheque for twice that for your trouble.'

He opened a big brown envelope he'd brought with him and handed it over. I stared at the contents. He meant what he'd said.

I'd been about to say – as kindly as possible – no way! I'm not who you need. But thirty grand upfront – a third of it in actual bank notes – made a difference. It made me even more patient and understanding.

I sat and thought for a few moments. And the more thought I gave it, the more things I could think of to do with the money. Most of them had something to do with the cottage, which seems to soak up energy and money like dry sand does water. Old properties, I have found, are like that.

'Where's Tom now?'

'In the car,' Josh said.

'Outside, you mean?' I asked with astonishment.

He nodded.

'We hoped you—' Anne began.

'Bring him in,' I said sharply to Josh. 'It's far too cold to be sitting out there.'

'You'll take the job?'

I nodded. 'I'll do my best.'

Josh got up, shook my hand and set off to bring his son in from the cold.

Anne, too, got to her feet. 'Thank you, Frank,' she said, kissing my cheek.

'Hey!' I protested, chuckling. 'That's the second time you've done that.'

She laughed and said, 'I haven't forgotten the first time either.'

I smiled and said, 'I have to ask you this, Anne. Why have you come to me with this problem? How did you even know what I do?'

'You were recommended.'

'Oh?'

'By a friend who has an art gallery in Middlesbrough.'

'Not Jac Picknett?'

She nodded, smiled and added, 'She said you would remember her.'

'Such conceit,' I murmured, shaking my head.

'Oh?' Anne looked at me mischievously, her head on one side. 'She implied you two were good together.'

'And so we were – once.'

'Like that, is it? Oh, well. But she still thinks a lot of you.'

'The feeling is mutual,' I assured her. 'Jac just doesn't like the way I live.'

Anne laughed at that. Perhaps it was funny. But for me it was a matter for regret.

Chapter Four

BLUE LIGHTS BEGAN flashing on the way back to base. Blue swore, hoping it was not them in the frame. But it was. The police car swerved in behind, closed up and flashed its headlights several times. There was no mistaking its meaning.

'What are we going to do?' Eddie asked. 'Run for it?'

Blue shook his head. The cop car was a Volvo, a highway patrol car. If it had been a little local panda he might have gone for it, but the Volvos were specially tuned and their drivers were trained for speed work.

'We can't outrun it,' he said, slowing to pull over. 'We'll tough it out. Cyril, you ready?'

'Sure am, boss man!'

Blue shook his head with irritation at the response. He stopped the car and got out. Then he stood with his back to the Volvo's lights, waiting. He heard the cop get out.

'Switch your engine off, sir, and get in my car, please.'

'What's the problem, officer?' Blue said, turning round and smiling.

Just the one man, he noted. That made it easier.

'Get in the car, please,' the cop said, opening the passenger side door.

'Speeding, was I? Missed a red light?'

The cop stepped closer.

'I don't believe you had any reason to stop me, officer,' Blue said, smiling still.

'Let me say it again, sir. Get in the car – please!'

Blue smiled pleasantly and stayed where he was.

Both back doors of their own car opened. Big Cyril slipped out quietly on the far side. Eddie got out on the near side, making a song and dance of it, stumbling and swearing. The cop ordered him back inside and became visibly agitated when Eddie failed to take any notice and instead stood close behind him. Blue kept talking.

The cop became even more agitated when the lights on the Volvo died. He spun round and started back, only to be tripped by Eddie.

As he scrabbled in the slushy snow to get back upright Blue pushed him down again with his foot. 'Stay there a minute,' he advised.

The cop ignored the advice and came up fighting. Blue doubled him up with a heavy blow to the belly. Then Eddie and Manny, helped by Chas, caught an arm apiece and dragged him behind the car and into the bushes beside the lay-by. Blue stood still, waiting, ignoring the grunts and thuds, until Cyril came back from the Volvo.

'Fixed the radio?'

'Fixed everything!' Big Cyril chuckled. 'Nothing electrical working now.'

Blue nodded. 'Put the cop in the back seat!' he called. 'Let's get out of here.'

'Give them a hand,' he said to Big Cyril when he saw the others were struggling with a dead weight.

As they drove away, Blue wondered why they had been stopped in the first place. There had been no reason for it that he could see.

'There's a back light not working,' Big Cyril said, as if he had heard the question in Blue's mind. 'I'll fix it when we get back.'

Blue grimaced and nodded. That was it, then. Question answered. A rear light. It could have been worse. 'Change the plates, as well,' he said over his shoulder. 'I want to hang on to this car. We've got more work to do.'

Chapter Five

TOM STEELE WAS a big, rangy lad. He came through the door apprehensively, as if he wasn't sure what he was being let in for. I felt something similar myself. What on earth was I going to do with him?

'He's taller than me now,' Josh said proudly.

I smiled at Tom and shook hands. 'How are you doing, Tom?'

'OK.' He shrugged and turned back to his father. 'What are we doing here?' he demanded.

'Frank has agreed to help. He's going to ... accompany you.'

'Yeah? Whatever that means,' he added, turning back to glower at me.

It wasn't the best of starts. I told myself things could only get better.

Anne joined in then. 'Tom, Frank is an old friend. He'll look after you for a week or two, until things calm down.'

'Look after me? What are his qualifications?' he asked scornfully.

'I don't have any certificates to show you, Tom,' I admitted, 'but I've been handling security work for some years now.'

'Security work? What, exactly? Fences, nightwatchman,

body-guarding?'

'All of that,' I said with a smile, 'and then some. Believe me, I really do have a lot of experience, both at home and abroad. It's how I make my living.'

He sneered, about to come back with some clever answer. His mother beat him to it. 'Frank comes highly recommended, Tom – by somebody I trust.'

'Yeah, yeah.'

I'd had about enough by then.

'Tell you what, Tom. If you think you can manage better on your own, you go right ahead, son. I can only help people who want to be helped.'

He shrugged and turned away. I looked at Josh.

'It'll be all right, Frank. He knows we need help.'

'I need to hear it from Tom. He's the one I'm going to be with.'

'Tom?' Anne said sharply.

'OK,' he said wearily. 'Whatever you want.'

I made us all some more coffee and then we discussed practical arrangements. Anne and Josh were quite certain what they wanted. They wanted me to take Tom away somewhere, and keep him out of harm's way for a couple of weeks. They didn't mind where we went. They just wanted Tom gone, and out of reach of the people threatening to do him harm.

The lad himself took no part in the discussions. He said he was tired and lapsed into a sullen silence in a far corner of the room. Feeling charitable, I put it down to stress.

'You obviously think you can solve this problem in a couple of weeks?' I suggested to his parents.

'We're working on it,' Josh said, nodding.

I waited but he said nothing more on that subject.

'Anything you need?' Josh asked.

I gave it a moment's thought.

'You said you have a car dealership. You wouldn't happen to have a spare car I can borrow, would you? All I have at the moment is the old Land Rover standing outside there. And if we're going to be travelling ...'

'That's your only vehicle?' Josh said, looking aghast.

'At the moment.'

'You need something better than that.'

'It's fine for around here,' I said defensively. 'I've been restoring it.'

Josh shook his head impatiently. 'What do you want? SUV? A four-wheel drive?'

'Nothing shiny-new and eye-catching. Tom and I are going to be sober, respectable citizens who don't attract attention.'

Anne chuckled.

After a moment, Josh smiled too. 'Maybe a used vehicle would suit you better?' he suggested. 'One with plates a year or two old?'

'Yes. That would be ideal.'

'I'll see what we've got. Better yet, come and choose for yourself.'

'Where?'

'Middlesbrough. We can go there now, if you like. Anything else you need?'

I shook my head.

'Let's get started then.'

Five minutes later we were on the road, all of us but the lad himself. Tom thought he would stay where he was and wait for me to return. I shrugged and said OK.

'Help yourself to anything you want, Tom,' I told him.

He nodded.

His mother said, 'Be good!'

He looked at her as if she came from another planet.

Back outside the front door, Josh paused and looked around for a moment. 'Interesting place you've got here, Frank,' he said. 'Kind of wild, but I can see the attraction.'

I wondered if he could. I really did. But at least he was being polite.

'It suits me,' I said with a shrug.

'Do you worry about the sea? Coastal erosion, and all that? What it might do to your cottage?'

'A little. The cliff edge gets closer every year.'

'And there's nothing to be done?'

I chuckled. 'Do I look like King Canute? Come on! Let's go.'

We dropped Anne off at the Steeles' home in Marton, just south of Middlesbrough. Their road was a tree-lined avenue of big, expensive houses, mostly built long ago when Teesside was an industrial power and the ironmasters preferred to live well away from the smoke their works created. We drove in through high ornamental gates that identified the car and opened automatically as we approached. Surveillance cameras watched us as we proceeded up the gravel drive. We stopped in front of a substantial red-brick house with big bay windows and lots of Virginia creeper covering the walls.

'Home,' Josh said with satisfaction.

I was impressed. 'Nice house.'

'Not bad, is it? Built in the 1920s by the owner of one of those big department stores they used to have in the town, long before our time. The guy knew what he was doing. Either that or his wife's designer did.'

'Come on,' Anne said. 'Let me out. I have things to do.'

Josh raised an eyebrow and grinned at me.

'Nice meeting you again, Frank,' she said. 'Look after Tom for me.'

'Don't worry about him,' I managed before she slammed the door shut.

'Let's go,' Josh said briskly, for all the world as if I was the one doing the driving.

Chapter Six

THE HOUSE WAS big, cold and damp. But it was also near enough to where they wanted to be yet well away from prying eyes. For the few weeks they needed it, this old farmhouse in the marshes was damn near perfect. At least, Blue thought so. For once, Logan had got something right.

'Shut up!' he snapped, when Chas started complaining again about what a dump it was. 'We've heard it all before.'

Chas visibly bristled. 'My best leather jacket! Ruined by mould.'

'Just shut it!' Blue said. 'Think of the money,' he added in a calmer tone. 'You'll be able to buy yourself a whole wardrobe full of leather jackets when this is over. You'll be Queen of the Ball!'

A couple of the others laughed.

Chas got to his feet, ready to take a swing at somebody. Blue caught him by the shoulders and forced him back down into his chair, exerting pressure that it would have taken a stronger man than Chas to resist. The heat went out of the moment. The tension died.

Blue spoke then to the whole group.

'Have a couple of beers, lads. You've done well tonight. Logan will be well pleased.'

'How many is a couple?' Manny asked with a grin.

'I don't think I need to spell it out,' Blue said, giving him the look. 'Do you?'

The grin subsided. Manny shook his head.

'I don't want anybody drunk tonight,' Blue continued. 'And no fighting! Whoever starts it will have me to reckon with. Clear?'

'Like the fucking army,' Chas muttered.

'And I'm the bloody sergeant major!' Blue growled. 'Don't you forget it. You're here to do a job. You're being well paid – and there's more to come, a lot more.'

'When we get the kid?' Eddie said.

'That's it.' Blue nodded. 'There's no way Logan will accept anything less. But before that happens, we've got a big day ahead of us.'

He ran his eyes around the group and added, 'Tomorrow we face the enemy. If it's fighting you want, you'll get plenty of that. You should be well satisfied by the end of tomorrow.'

Chapter Seven

AFTER DROPPING ANNE off we drove to Middlesbrough, and through the former Ironmasters District beside the river, the spot where the town began life nearly two hundred years ago.

'Where are we going?'

Josh grinned and said, 'You'll see.'

I would have preferred him just to tell me but he was intent on doing it his own way. Now we were back on his territory, and he was in control, he seemed much happier and more relaxed. Perhaps just being away from Anne helped. She seemed to know where to stick the knives.

For myself, I didn't want any diversions, or to be involved in any little family games. I just wanted to get on with the job. Every minute I was not with Tom, the lad was vulnerable. But I needed a car. So I had to do it Josh's way.

There were no blast furnaces or forges in the Ironmasters District now. No streets of terraced houses in the old St Hilda's ward to go with them either. Most of the area north of the railway – the historic 'Border' separating the oldest and the poorest parts of the town from the rest – was flattened and semi-derelict now, and had been for many years. Regeneration had started long ago but it had stalled and still had far to go, the modern football stadium and a big new building for the local college notwithstanding. It hadn't been helped by the recent economic recession either.

Employment-wise, there were a few scrapyards and recycling facilities in the area, vultures at the tail-end of the industrial revolution. There were also a number of small and newish, or converted, industrial buildings where some work was being done. But a big housing project looked to have been waylaid by the banking crisis. Signs of new life? Spring shoots? Yes, but ... How you saw it all depended on whether your glass was half full or half empty.

Josh chuckled and glanced at me. 'Remember what that train journey used to be like, Frank? Redcar to Middlesbrough?'

'In the good old days, you mean? Roaring furnaces, belching smoke and steam, flames and clouds of cinders on either side?'

'That's the one!'

I could just remember it, from when I was a kid. The railway used to come right through the middle of all the works along the south side of the river.

'Hell on earth!' Josh grinned and added, 'But jobs, as well, remember?'

'For the men of steel. We wouldn't want them now, though, would we?'

'Some of us didn't want them even then!'

He laughed. Then he changed gear and slowed down.

'Where's this?' I asked suspiciously as he turned into a big compound surrounded by high heavy-duty security fencing.

'My place,' he said. 'One of them, I should say. Mostly used specialist vehicles here, but there's a range of more ordinary cars, as well, if that's what you want.'

We parked outside an office building. A man dressed like an undertaker in a dark suit rushed across to greet us effusively.

'Mr Steele! How good to see you, sir.'

Josh treated him to a weary smile. 'This is Mr Doy, Gerald,' he said, when he could get a word in. 'He's here to find himself a vehicle.'

'Very well, Mr Steele,' Gerald said with enthusiasm. He beamed at me and thrust out a hand that I had to take for a moment. 'Welcome, Mr Doy!' he exclaimed, seizing my hand and pumping my arm vigorously.

I nodded, reclaimed my arm and surreptitiously wiped the palm of my hand on my trouser leg. I couldn't help it.

'Frank,' Josh said, 'why don't you look around the yard? See if there's anything that takes your fancy. I'll be in the office when you're done.'

He turned then and headed off with Gerald, evidently confident that left to my own devices I would find what I wanted.

I stood and looked around for a moment, wondering if I

shouldn't just take the Land Rover after all. This was all taking time, too much time. While we were messing about here, nobody was protecting Tom, and from what I'd seen of the lad he wasn't capable of looking after himself.

Common sense got the better of me. I needed something that would go faster and further than the Land Rover, and provide more comfort. Most of all, I needed something that wasn't going to break down every few miles. The Land Rover was my unfinished restoration project. Sometimes I wondered if it would ever get any better than it was right now.

Josh's yard was an Aladdin's cave of a place. I wandered around for a few minutes, getting a feel for it. I could see that it really was a showroom for specialist vehicles. There were cars there that I had never seen before, as well as cars of which I had only ever had fleeting glimpses. Specialist marques. Sports cars, four-by-fours, luxury saloons, truly fast cars. Some new, most used. I walked past the BMWs and Mercedes, the Porsches and the one Aston Martin. I didn't even bother looking at the Bentley or the Lotus.

On the far side, an open gate gave access to another compound, this one stocked with a range of industrial vehicles and giant machines. Trucks. Big generators. Pumps. Cranes. Mechanical diggers. Tractors. A couple of men were busy loading a massive tractor and a combine harvester onto a suitably enormous wagon bearing Hungarian plates. Nearby, other men were working on a huge machine that looked as if it would only be truly happy when spraying tarmac on a motorway or airport runway. Beyond them stood a vast hangar carrying advertising for offshore supplies and services.

I was impressed. All in all, Josh's yard was quite a place. It was on the riverside, as well, and had its own jetty, I noted. That must come in handy. It would be hard to move some of this stuff by road. Far easier by sea. At one time, not too long ago, the entire property would have been occupied by a steelworks. Then the jetty would have been handy for offloading iron ore and coal, and for onloading pig-iron, steel rails and whatever else was made here. Now it was being put to another use. Good for Josh.

I wandered over towards the river and smiled when I saw the name on a coaster tied up at the jetty: ss *Anne*. Their own ship even!

I returned to the first compound and found what I wanted over against a distant fence where the also-rans were gathered, the cars that wouldn't excite collectors or speed freaks. It was a dirty, red Volvo S80 with ten thousand miles on the clock, and four-wheel drive if you needed it. Ideal.

It wasn't a car to attract admiring glances. In fact, it was a pretty dull-looking machine. But it was well engineered. I knew a lot of police forces liked to have that model for their fast, motorway drivers, which made it good enough for me. I didn't think I would want to be travelling at much more than 150 mph. And having a few miles on the clock meant that it would be well run-in, any teething problems long since ironed out.

Josh looked surprised for a moment when I told him what I wanted. Then he just nodded. He didn't question my choice or offer any advice.

'I'll tell Gerald to get it serviced, cleaned and delivered,' he said crisply. 'It will be with you first thing in the morning, weather permitting.'

I shook my head. 'Not cleaned, Josh. Not on the outside, at least. I don't want that.'

He stared at me a moment and then nodded again. 'All right, Frank. You're the expert. Nothing to attract attention, eh?'

'That's right.'

'OK. Gerald will have it dropped off at your place when it's ready. Are you likely to be taking it abroad? I'm thinking about foreign-use documents.'

'I don't think so.'

Josh pursed his lips judiciously and said, 'I'll have him sort the documentation out anyway, just in case.'

'OK. Thanks.'

If Gerald could get all that done, and get the car to me at Risky Point by first thing in the morning, I could understand why Josh tolerated him.

As we left the depot, I asked about the compound with the heavy equipment.

'It's a separate business. Plant hire, and some sales.'

'Overseas sales as well?' I asked, thinking of the Hungarian wagon.

'Some, yes.'

'And offshore supplies and servicing? Quite an empire you have here, Josh.'

'Isn't it?' he said, throwing me a little smile.

'Well protected, too,' I added, having noted the fencing and lights, and the uniformed security staff.

'It's necessary,' he said with a grimace. 'If this lot went up, we'd be finished. Fortunately, no one has broken in here yet. But our timber compound at South Bank went up in flames last night.'

'Really?'

He nodded. 'A million quid's worth. Even with the insurance, I'll lose a packet on that. Then there's the disruption it will cause to my construction business.'

'Construction, too?' The empire was even bigger than I had realized.

'You need better security – everywhere.'

'Welcome aboard!' Josh said, throwing me a rueful smile. 'But you just keep Tom safe, Frank. I'll settle for that.'

Chapter Eight

So far, so good. Everything well organized and provided for, and a nice little away trip in prospect. Just what I needed, especially as it was one that would earn me some decent money. I would have a sullen teenager in tow, true, but I wasn't too worried about that. I was confident he would soon come round. All that was really on my mind was getting back to Risky Point, starting the job and getting Tom out of the danger zone.

Then things changed.

We were no sooner through the gates than Josh's phone went into Swedish Rhapsody. He took the call, using the hands-free setup, and Anne's voice suddenly filled the car.

'Josh! The house is under attack!' she shrieked. 'Masked men! I'm going to the panic room.'

'Stay there!' Josh shouted.

He stopped the car and punched in a speed-dial number. 'Get to the house now, Marty! Anne's under attack.'

He switched off and got the car moving again, racing through the gears, making the engine scream. I was stunned and said nothing for a moment, wondering if I'd misheard or misunderstood.

'Trouble – big trouble,' Josh snapped, his face set in a grim expression.

I pulled out my phone.

'What are you doing?' he demanded.

'Calling the police.'

'Leave it!'

I hesitated, thumbs poised over the keys.

'Leave it, Frank! I don't want them involved.'

'Anne's in danger, for crissake!'

'No police. I'll explain later.'

I stared at him a moment. Then I shrugged and reluctantly put the phone away. It was his call.

By then, we were travelling at an unsustainable speed for a town centre, especially one deep in slushy snow and no doubt with hidden patches of ice on the road. Josh was weaving through the traffic, dodging a bus here, ignoring a red light there – and taking absolutely no notice at all of the car horns blaring in protest. I braced myself for the moment we skidded off the road or hit something bigger than us.

'Slow down, Josh!'

He kept going for a few seconds more before he relented. Then he glanced at the speedometer and eased his foot back slightly. The speed dropped to sixty, still enough to attract half the police in Cleveland. Maybe that was the idea. Get them to follow us back to the house. Great plan!

'The house is under attack?' I shouted again over the roar of the engine.

'They're after Tom.'

'And Anne's in a panic room?'

He nodded. He volunteered nothing more and I didn't ask. I preferred him to concentrate on his driving. I wanted to survive the journey.

But, still. A panic room?

It took us fifteen minutes to get there; a long time for a lone woman in a house under siege, but a world record to my way of thinking.

Just before we arrived Josh said, 'It's that bastard, Logan!'

I looked at him.

'The guy,' he added.

The bereaved father, I assumed he meant. So that was his name. Logan. It meant nothing to me.

'He's gone over the top this time,' Josh growled.

That seemed to qualify for understatement of the year. I thought now of Anne, and wondered how many business-people on Teesside had a panic room in their home. I'd never come across any. It made the Steeles seem pretty special.

The signs of an assault in progress were not hard to spot as we roared up the drive in a shower of gravel. The front door had been smashed off its hinges and the adjacent windows were gaping holes. There seemed to be broken glass everywhere.

Josh skidded to a stop and we spilled out onto the gravelled forecourt. Suddenly men were milling about in the doorway and falling out of the house, locked in combat. People were screaming and shouting, in anger and in pain.

As Josh came round the front of the car, a big guy in combat fatigues rushed at him, raising a tyre lever above his head. I knocked Josh aside and grabbed the raised arm. A knee came up towards my groin. I twisted out of the way and rammed an elbow into the big guy's face. He fell back. I pulled his weapon away and hit him with it. Once was enough. His arm was broken. He screamed, and turned and fled.

I glanced at Josh, who was just getting back to his feet. 'All right?'

He nodded and peered around, visibly shocked. 'Thanks, Frank. What the hell...?'

I missed the rest of it as I spun round, waiting for the next attack. It didn't happen. The space in front of the house was suddenly clearing. Men were running into the shrubbery, disappearing amongst the rhododendrons and conifers, with other men chasing them. There were screams and yells of triumph. Absolute pandemonium. It was like a film set for a battle scene. I'd never seen anything like it.

I didn't know what to do next either. There was no point joining in. I didn't know the good guys from the bad. I didn't know anybody – or anything!

A car raced up the drive behind us. I readied myself for an attack, but the occupants were two women. Josh held up a hand to hold them back. Then we both headed for the house.

A tough-looking man in a black boiler suit had stationed himself in the doorway, wielding a baseball bat in both hands, ready to swing.

'Did they get to my wife?' Josh shouted.

Fortunately, the doorman seemed to recognize him. 'No. She's OK.'

'Did you catch any of them?'

The man just shrugged and pointed into the shrubbery. How the hell would he know?

'Marty inside?'

'Yeah.'

Josh charged past him into the house. I followed, not sorry that we seemed to be a bit late for the main battle. The aftermath was something to see: overturned furniture, shelves swept clear of ornaments, broken chairs, a big-screen TV with a curtain pole sticking out of it. Display cabinets and a dresser had been toppled over, their contents spilled across rugs and a hardwood floor. Doors were off their hinges. Somehow a huge hole had been smashed through the dining room wall. The place was a spectacular mess.

But the news, and the situation, wasn't all bad. At least Tom was well out of it. And whoever the attackers were, they hadn't reached Anne either.

A couple of men in black boiler suits, like the one at the door, were gazing around as if they, too, were wondering what the hell had just happened. Josh rushed past them with scarcely a glance, heading for a flight of stairs off the kitchen.

I followed him down into a basement, where we joined a couple of other men who were talking to Anne. It looked as if she had just emerged from the reinforced concrete bunker behind her that seemed to serve as the panic room.

Anne turned as we clattered down the stairs. She gave Josh a look that was hard to interpret. Anger? Disdain? Whatever. But it was pretty clear who she blamed for all this.

'Are you all right, love?' he asked, taking hold of her.

'Of course.'

She seemed remarkably calm. Not unruffled, but poised and in control. Haughty even. Definitely not collapsed in a heap. She allowed him to hug her momentarily and then pulled back.

'Marty, this is Frank Doy,' Josh said to the tall, lean man standing closest to Anne. 'He's helping us.'

Marty looked at me and nodded, but didn't say anything.

'Marty's my security chief,' Josh told me.

I felt like a spare part. But that was all right. Babysitting Tom was what I'd signed up for, not countering home invasions. This wasn't where I needed to be.

'You got here in good time?' Josh asked Marty.

'Two or three minutes after you called.' Marty shrugged. 'There was a bit of a scrap. Then they pulled out.'

All in a day's work, obviously. I found myself wondering if Josh needed Marty and his men often. It must be some business he had.

'Any casualties?' Josh pressed.

'Us or them?' Marty asked with a grin.

Josh just waited. He wasn't in the mood for jokes.

'There'll be some. But I don't really know yet. I'll have to check.'

Josh nodded and whirled round, distracted. He wanted to do something – hit somebody, probably.

'Do you want me to get Gerald to come out and clear the house up?' Marty asked.

Josh said he did. Then he suggested to Anne and me that we all went back upstairs, which we did. By then I was thinking this was more like gang warfare than a case of a distraught father trying to avenge a dead son. Was it really all about Tom? I was finding that increasingly hard to believe.

Chapter Nine

I STOOD AROUND at a loose end for a while as Josh and Anne did some damage assessment. The bill was going to be considerable, I couldn't help thinking. Without setting fire to the place, or machine-gunning or bombing it, little more could have been done by the invaders in such a short time.

'Don't worry so much,' I heard Anne say. 'Gerald will soon get it sorted.'

Josh seemed appeased by that suggestion. It made me think Gerald must be a handy guy to have around. Selfishly, I also wondered if this new situation would prevent him sorting out the car for me and Tom, as promised.

'Who are you?'

I spun round.

'Hello!' I said to the good-looking young woman who had crept up on me. I had no idea where she'd come from.

She wore her dark hair long and stood very tall and straight, poised on her toes like a high-jumper about to tackle a high bar. There was a wild, feisty look in her eye.

'You are?' she insisted.

'Let's just say I'm a friend of the family,' I said with a smile. 'And you?'

'What are you doing here?' she demanded, ignoring my question.

'I was invited.'

'I don't think so! Stay right where you are. Don't move.' She spun round and called, 'Josh! Josh, over here.'

I had no idea what might happen if I did move. Maybe I would get my head kicked in. I could see she was deadly serious.

Before Josh could respond to the summons, there was a disturbance in the hall. Loud voices and the crash of heavy feet on polished floor. Then a couple of police uniforms burst into the room, followed by DI Bill Peart, my old friend and occupational sparring partner from the Cleveland Force.

Bill and I stared at each other.

'What are you doing here?' he demanded.

'I'm wondering that myself,' I said with a shrug. 'How about you?'

He frowned impatiently. 'Where's the owner of the house?'

I pointed towards the kitchen.

'Stay where you are,' he instructed, pointing a warning finger. 'Don't move! I'll be right back.'

So now there were two of them giving me orders.

Anne reappeared, looking very angry now. I wondered if Josh had blotted his copy book again or if it was the police incursion that had tipped her over the edge.

'What's going on?' I asked.

'A neighbour tipped them off, apparently,' she said bitterly. 'There's always somebody sticking their nose in.'

It seemed an odd comment, given what had just happened here. But, then again, it wasn't my home that had been trashed. She had every right to feel aggrieved about something.

'I'm very sorry this has happened, Anne.' I glanced around and grimaced. 'It's not nice, is it?'

'Oh, we'll soon have it sorted,' she said with a shrug. 'Just you make sure they don't get to Tom.'

A blonde girl, another new arrival, headed towards us.

'The last thing I need!' Anne whispered fiercely.

'Where's Tom?' the girl said plaintively. 'Where is he?'

'Not now, Julie,' Anne said. 'Please. You've come at a bad time.'

The girl looked around, as if noticing for the first time that things were a bit amiss.

'What's going on?' she asked even more plaintively. 'Why can't I see Tom?'

'Tom's not here, Julie,' Anne said patiently. 'If he was, you could see him.'

'I'll wait for him,' the girl decided.

'Not here,' Anne said firmly. 'Apart from anything else, the police have arrived.'

'The police? Oh, God!'

Julie hurried away.

I looked at Anne and raised my eyebrows.

'I know, I know,' she said wearily. 'It's how we seem to live these days.'

I kept my counsel.

Then I saw the tall, long-haired woman reappear and head

determinedly our way.

'Who's this?' I asked. 'Another one?'

'My sister, Senga,' Anne said with a giggle.

The sister came straight up to me. 'I told you!' she began angrily.

'Hello, Senga,' I said with a smile. 'I'm so pleased to meet you.'

That stopped her. She scowled and looked from me to Anne, and back again.

'This is Frank Doy,' Anne said gently. 'Frank's an old friend.'

'Why didn't you say so?' the woman said, glowering at me.

'You didn't really give me the chance.'

I received another fierce glare. Then she turned and walked away.

'Don't mind Senga,' Anne said. 'She's upset.'

I nodded and didn't bother asking what she was upset about. Anne had more important questions to address. Actually, I was a little disappointed Senga and I had got off to such a bad start. If anything, she was even better looking than Anne.

Soon afterwards, Josh told one of Marty's lads to drive me home. He apologized for not doing it himself, but said he and Anne had too much to do. I was OK with that. In fact, I wasn't sorry to get out of there and away from the Steeles. I needed to get my head around what had happened. Not only the violence, but also why they didn't want the police involved. I had stepped into a situation that was hard to fathom, and it was worrying.

Senga followed us outside.

'Help you?' I said.

She stared at me for a moment, seemed about to say something and then shook her head and walked back inside. Clearly, I wasn't worth bothering with. The feeling of being a spare part came back to me very strongly.

Chapter Ten

'So how did it go?'

'We got kicked out.'

'Say again.'

'We made a strategic withdrawal, on account of how we didn't have enough manpower to sustain the fight.'

That set him off. Blue grinned and held the phone away from his ear for a moment.

When he'd calmed down, Logan said, 'I hope the guys you did have gave a good account of themselves?'

'They did great.'

'Any casualties?'

'One or two. You don't need to know about them, though.'

'Indeed I don't. I take it you're OK? I don't need a new Chief of Staff?'

'Not yet, no.'

'So what else?'

'There's this guy they visited yesterday. We're going to pay him a call.'

'What guy? Who is he? What is he?'

'Some sort of private eye.'

'You're kidding!'

'Wish I was. We're going to warn him off.'

'Agreed. We don't want him getting in the way and messing things up. Make your visit count. What about the kid?'

'He wasn't there.'

'Pity.'

'We'll get him. Sooner or later, we will. He's only been out a couple of days, remember?'

'Even so, I don't want to hang about over this. I want it done.

Then we can move on.'

Blue thought soon he would be moving on himself anyway. A few more days and it would be the end of the month. All this shit with the Steeles was more a distraction than anything else, so far as he was concerned. He could do without it.

But he had to keep Logan sweet for now. He needed him. Better to help Logan get what he wanted, in order to get what he himself wanted – and absolutely had to have.

'You should have snatched the wife,' Logan said belatedly. 'Even if she didn't know where the kid is, she could still have been useful.'

'We never saw her. She disappeared before we got into the house, and when we did get in we couldn't find her.'

'You can't have looked hard enough.'

'Believe me – we looked! Then a whole fucking army arrived. We had to fight our way out.'

'But the boys did all right?' Logan said, backing down.

'Pretty good. Steele's lot will know they were in a fight. The house will take some clearing up, as well,' Blue added with a chuckle.

'Well, we're not going to stop now,' Logan growled. 'We'll keep going.'

Sometimes Blue wondered how much the kid counted. Oh, he did count. But how much, compared with everything else at stake? It was hard to know.

The phone went dead, call ended. Blue glanced at it and swore softly. He'd like to jam the damned thing down Logan's throat.

'Problem, boss?' Eddie asked.

Blue shook his head. 'Just the usual. Nothing I can't handle.'

He hoped that was actually true. With Logan, you couldn't be sure. You never could quite tell. On the other hand, he was pretty sure Logan knew there were limits to how far he could go. There were times when it was worth remembering that. It helped keep the peace.

From the driveway of a house on the other side of the road, a little further along the street, they could see the entrance to the Steele property through the giant cypresses and the rampant azaleas and rhododendrons. There was plenty of activity. Cars, including police vehicles, were going in and stacking up on the driveway and the forecourt outside the house.

'Here's one coming out,' Eddie said.

Blue looked up. It was a big Mitsubishi SUV, the first vehicle they had seen leaving the premises. As it passed, he peered hard at the two occupants and swore. Then he called Logan again.

'That PI Steele went to see has just been driven away from the house. So he must be involved now. He's being taken somewhere.'

'Steele with him?'

'No. He'll be busy sorting his house out.'

'Follow the guy. See where he lives.'

'We already know that.'

'Well, you know what to do – just do it!'

Indeed he did know, Blue thought, switching off. It should be fun.

Chapter Eleven

Tom was more or less where we'd left him, sitting in a corner, glancing without much interest at a picture book about Norway he had plucked from a shelf.

'Everything all right, Tom?'

'Yeah.'

I decided not to tell him about the fracas at the family home. Time enough for that later. The news wouldn't cheer him up much.

'Your dad's having a car delivered first thing in the morning,' I told him. 'My old Land Rover isn't the most comfortable of vehicles in this sort of weather.'

'Right.'

'I just need to make a couple of phone calls. Then we can have an early night, and be ready to take off as soon as the car arrives.'

He nodded, without seeming to have much interest in what I was saying or what we were going to do. I was beginning to wonder if he suffered from depression. He certainly had a lot of the symptoms. Then again, he had a lot to be depressed about.

I had to admit, I was worried about him. Given what we were going to be doing, I wanted him sharp and alert. I didn't want a somnolent passenger without any interest in what was happening around us. I couldn't do everything myself.

'So nothing's happened while I've been away?'

He shook his head. Then he changed his mind and said, 'Some old guy came by for you. I said you weren't in.'

'Who was it? Did he say?'

Tom shook his head again. 'Some old fisherman gadgy.'

I described Jimmy Mack, and Tom decided that had been him.

'What did he want?'

'No idea,' Tom said with a yawn. 'I just told him to piss off.'

'In that case, you're lucky you didn't have a marline spike

rammed down your throat.'

He looked slightly concerned about that, which was a welcome change.

'Jimmy Mack,' I said gently, 'is my only neighbour, as well as my friend. He lives next door. If you really said that to him, you'd better apologize.'

'Yeah, well.'

I left it at that, but I was having difficulty with Tom's general attitude. He was stressed, I told myself. Leave him be a bit longer.

While I cooled down, I rang a guy I knew who had a couple of holiday cottages he hired out. No problem, Pete said. The business was welcome, especially at this time of year.

'You're into skiing or ice fishing, I take it?' he added.

'Cold, is it? No, I just want somewhere quiet and out of the way for a week or two. That's all.'

'You're going to the right place, in that case,' Pete said with a chuckle. 'I keep saying to the wife it was the worst thing we ever did, buying them cottages. Nobody wants to go there, except in July and August. Or when we get one of them once-in-a-century heatwaves in March or December.'

'It should suit me fine.'

I wrote down the address and navigation instructions, promised to put a cheque in the post and ended the call feeling I'd made some progress.

Tom wasn't in a talkative mood. So I showed him the spare bedroom and where everything was. He seemed happy to take himself off to bed after that, and I was glad to have some time to myself. I needed some thinking time after everything that had happened. I was unsure what I'd got myself into. It had seemed so straightforward at first, but I could see now it was a long way from being that.

Things didn't seem good between Mr and Mrs Steele, for one thing. That was a worry. They were my client, and a client divided can be awkward. Who do you listen to?

Then there was Tom. He and I were going to have some long, dreary days ahead of us if his attitude didn't change. We didn't have to be best pals but we ought to be able to have pleasant, sensible conversations.

The biggest worry of all, though, was that the Steeles seemed to have found themselves some serious trouble. They were up against a real bunch of desperadoes, if the attacks on their properties and even their home were evidence. Yet they had resented the arrival of the police; didn't want them involved at all. Why was that?

It worried me. Any normal businesspeople in their situation would have been out there demanding a police presence and complaining about lack of protection. Did the Steeles really think they could handle it themselves? Or did they have things to hide?

In any case, what were they going to do to protect themselves if they didn't want the police involved? Beef up their private army – Marty and the boys – to ward off further attacks, and deal their enemy a mortal blow? Or were they going to try to pay him off? That might be a safer option, although there was no guarantee it would work if avenging Logan's dead son was what it was all about.

But was it? I wasn't even sure about that now. They seemed to have something in mind but I didn't know them well enough to be able to guess what it was. I decided to concentrate on what they had asked me to do, and leave the rest to them. I had no choice, really.

Looking after Tom for a week or two was going to be enough

for me anyway. It would keep us both out of the way – and avoid incurring the wrath of Bill Peart for interfering – as well as earning me some much needed dosh.

Having got that far, I gave up and went to bed. I hadn't thought any more about Anne's sister or the other, younger woman, Julie. They just seemed to be part of the general craziness around the Steele family.

It was hard and cold the next morning before the sun came up. Frost had settled on the land and given the snow cover an icy crust. Pockets of fog had sunk into the hollows, and puffs of it were swirling around the cliff top. The sea was impressed enough to be doing no more than quietly murmur in the background.

God, it was cold! My Land Rover looked as if it had come out of the freezer. Just as well I didn't need it. It takes some starting on mornings like that. I was looking forward to the arrival of Josh's car.

The snow crunched beneath my feet as I walked over to the shed to collect a snow shovel, thinking I would clear a parking space for the car. Before I started work, I paused to blow warm air into my cupped hands.

It was then that I saw the first of them. A hundred yards or so away stood a motionless figure, its legs wreathed in fog, seemingly staring at me. My heart began to beat faster.

My eyes moved sideways and I spotted another figure, also immobile, and also staring at me. My eyes moved on and I spotted more. Altogether there were six of them. None moving. All looking my way. They formed a loose, menacing circle at a distance around the cottage, their very stillness extraordinarily sinister.

It didn't look good. My grip on the snow shovel tightened. I assumed they'd come for Tom, but how did they know he was here?

When I heard feet crunching through the frozen snow I turned to look along the approach track to the cottage. A heavy-set man I'd never seen before was walking steadily towards me. Beyond him were two parked vehicles that must have brought my visitors.

I studied the approaching man. If he came alone, I could deal with him. If all of them started moving in together, I was going back inside for my shotgun. No messing. I might not be the brightest star in the sky, but I can count up to six, seven even, and I know when I'm outnumbered.

But for now, I just waited.

The man walking along the track drew steadily closer. He could have driven to my door. The others could have waited in their vehicles, or closed in with him. But no. They stayed where they were, alarmingly still and threatening.

Then it struck me. Something about this wasn't real. It was … fantasy. Somebody understood the power of theatre, and was using it to try to frighten me.

I walked out onto the track and stood facing the approaching man. I could see now that he wasn't young. Maybe in his forties. He looked big and powerful, and he had tidy, short black hair. Despite the temperature that morning, he wore only jeans and a checked work shirt, with the sleeves rolled up. I wondered if that was to demonstrate his strength or to let me see he was not armed. Having said that, he looked like someone who wouldn't normally need weapons to get his way.

But this wasn't the first time trouble had walked up to my door. I wasn't someone easily intimidated, and I wasn't going to back down now. I stood my ground, facing him, and waited.

He came to a halt when he was a couple of yards away. He stared hard, his eyes boring into me, his expression blank.

'Mr Doy,' he said in a low growl, 'you'd be well advised to keep out of things that don't concern you. Have nothing to do with the Steele family. Turn down any job offer they make. Refuse to accept their money. Have nothing to do with them. Is that clear?'

I nodded, having pretended to think about it. 'And you are?'

'Have nothing to do with them,' he repeated, ignoring my question. 'Take a holiday. Visit a sick aunt. Just keep out of the way. Then you'll be safe.'

'They with you?' I asked, turning to look round at the figures in the landscape.

He didn't deign to reply. I stared at each of them in turn, making a point of it. 'I'll assume they are. You're on private land, you know. My advice to you is to get off it.'

'I give people fair warning before I take further action,' my visitor said, undeflected. 'That saves a lot of bother and heartache. Unnecessary trouble, too,' he added, as if I might be a slow learner.

'I don't frighten easily,' I told him with a smile I didn't find easy to muster. 'I'm not intimidated by any of this.'

'You should be. This is the only warning you'll get.'

He turned and walked away, heading back towards the vehicles. The figures in the landscape began moving, too, as if he had pulled unseen strings to jerk them back into life.

It was impressive in its way, the performance, but it was still theatre of the absurd. Making sense of it was going to be a challenge.

Chapter Twelve

'WHAT DID THEY want?' Tom demanded when I got back inside.

'Oh, you're up, are you? Nothing. Don't worry about it.'

He was hovering on the stairs, looking agitated.

'They were after me, weren't they? What did you tell them?'

I shut the front door firmly and made for the kitchen. 'Let's have some breakfast, Tom, now you're up.'

'I hope you didn't sell me out,' he said bitterly.

'I'm going to pretend you didn't say that, Tom. Now what do you want to eat? Let's get started. It's going to be a long day.'

He sat on the stairs, staring at me belligerently. 'What did you tell them?'

'Nothing, nothing at all. If it makes you feel any better, they don't even know you're here.'

I didn't add that if they had known they would probably just have come in and taken him – or shot him. I wouldn't have been able to stop them.

'They were Logan's men, presumably?' I said.

'Yeah. The guy you were talking to is called Blue.'

'Blue?'

'Don't ask me. I know nothing about him, except he's a hard bastard.'

'Unusual name. Is that his surname or a nickname?'

'No idea.' Tom shrugged. 'It's all he ever gets called.'

He descended the stairs, apparently satisfied that I hadn't sold him out, and we were able to get on with breakfast.

Once again, though, I had the sense that everyone else knew more than I did. How, for instance, did Tom know about this guy Blue? I'd never heard him mentioned before.

*

50

A little later Jimmy Mack wanted to show me something. He came over soon after we had finished eating and had me walk back to his place with him. His cottage is significantly closer than mine to the cliff edge.

Not now, Jim! I was thinking. I assumed he was going to complain about Tom, and I really hadn't got time for that. I was itching to get moving. But I went with him because the car still hadn't arrived and I wanted to placate him.

I was wrong about what he wanted.

'There!' Jimmy said, as soon as we were inside his living room. He pointed at the far wall. 'It happened in the early hours.'

I peered at the wall and saw what he meant. A long horizontal crack had appeared since my last visit, twenty-four hours earlier. It zigzagged from one side of the room to the other.

I grimaced. 'It's new, isn't it?'

He didn't bother replying.

I moved up close and studied the crack. It wasn't good, for either of us. I poked a finger into the plaster and met resistance. 'It doesn't go all the way through,' I pointed out.

'Not yet.' Jimmy shrugged and added, 'But it'll be a toss-up which goes first, the cottage or me.'

I shook my head and chuckled uneasily. 'I shouldn't worry about it, Jim. It's just a crack in the plaster. No need to panic.'

'It means the ground has shifted,' he said stubbornly. 'It was like that just before the last two cottages went.'

I shrugged. 'So what do you want to do?'

'Stop here, I suppose,' he said. 'Be the last man standing.'

'So you just wanted to upset my morning by showing me this crack?'

He grinned. There was nothing more to be said. He had just wanted to share the problem, and halve the load.

'I'm going away for a while, Jim. When I get back, I'll see

what we can do.'

'You're going to hold the cliff up, are you?'

'With your help.'

He chuckled, but his heart wasn't in it. I knew how he felt.

I left him to it. I had other things, more immediate things, to worry about. But I knew he might well be right. The cliff could be preparing for another collapse, another retreat. And if Jimmy went, I would be the last man standing.

An hour later, by which time the sun had lit up Cleveland in its white blanket to look like Switzerland, Gerald's men arrived in two cars. One turned an Audi round and waited. The other parked the Volvo I had selected, got out and came over to me. He handed over the keys and a packet of documents.

'Sorry we couldn't get here any earlier,' he said. 'There was a problem sourcing a coil spring for the suspension. Everything's done now, though. And Gerald says you've got the documentation to go abroad, if you need it. There's also a road atlas and a satnav in the car.'

I nodded my thanks and riffled quickly through the documents. Log book, insurance, breakdown cover. I couldn't see that anything was missing. They had done very well getting all this together and sorting the car out overnight, especially given the chaos at the house. I took my hat off to Gerald.

'Good luck,' the delivery man said. 'And don't forget your passport!' he added with a grin as he turned away.

I watched him get into the passenger seat of the Audi, and I watched the car pull smoothly away. A glimpse of long hair suggested the driver was a woman. Once the car was on the main road I turned and went back inside, wondering who the driver was. From the brief glimpse I'd had, it could have been Anne Steele's stroppy sister, Senga.

Then the phone went.

'I thought I told you to stay where you were. I wanted to speak to you.'

'Morning, Bill!'

'Is it? So what happened?'

I grimaced and took the phone over to the window. I thought the tranquil view might help me keep my temper with Bill Peart. We would both have too much to lose if angry words got the better of us.

'I didn't think I was under arrest,' I said calmly. 'In fact, I don't see how I could have been. I'd only just arrived.'

'What were you doing there?'

He was being particularly awkward this morning. He must have had a bad night, or not been to bed at all, perhaps.

'The Steeles had asked me to do some work for them.'

'What? Find out who wrecked their house?'

I chuckled. 'That's your job, isn't it?'

'It is now.'

I heard the tension go out of him with a sigh. Perhaps he had remembered at last that I was a friend.

'So how did that happen?' I asked.

'I was the only one free when a call from the neighbour came in.'

'And at calls from that road, with all those posh houses, you jump, eh? That's if you like your job, and want to keep it, of course.'

'Very funny. Did you see who broke into the house?'

'No. It was all over by the time me and Josh Steele arrived. The wife was there all the time, though.'

'So I understand. In a bloody panic room, would you believe! Hell of a set up they've got there. I've never seen anything like it.'

'Me neither.'

He sighed again, considered things and decided there was nothing more he wanted to say to me just then. His parting shot was, 'I'll drop by later and see what you can tell me about these people.'

'It's not a good time, Bill.'

'I'll drop by anyway.'

The phone went dead. I shook my head. I deliberately hadn't bothered telling him I wouldn't be here. He might have stopped me and Tom leaving.

'Come on, Tom,' I said, looking round at my guest. 'Let's get out of here.'

'We're leaving?'

'Yeah.'

'When?'

'Right now.'

Chapter Thirteen

MOVING WAS GOOD. It took my mind off all the problems I couldn't solve or get out of my head.

I was happy, happy-ish at least, with what I'd been recruited to do. Getting Tom out of harm's way was something I could handle, and was worth doing. It was all the other stuff that really bothered me. The sheer scale of the vendetta against the Steeles, for one thing. And the antagonism – hostility at times – between Tom's parents. Plus their antipathy towards the police.

That last consideration, together with Tom being able to

name the guy he said was called Blue, added to my feeling that the Steeles knew a lot more about their persecutor, Logan, than they had been prepared to tell me. That was worrying. What had I got myself into?

Whatever it was, there was nothing I could do about it at that moment. So I concentrated on the driving, and hoped my time away with Tom would provide some of the answers I wanted.

I dropped down to the A171, the main road to and from Whitby, and turned to head for Guisborough on the southern edge of Teesside, or the 'Tees Valley' as we are being encouraged to call the area in its post-industrial incarnation. The ploughs and gritters had been out in force overnight and we hadn't had any more snow. So the road wasn't too bad now. We were able to travel at a reasonable speed.

Tom still seemed uninterested in what we were doing and where we were going. Most of the time he spent fiddling with his mobile phone; texting, it looked like. I let him be for a while.

My thoughts turned to the theatrical performance on my doorstep that morning. What had that been about? It appeared that Logan felt I was a threat to his plans. I wasn't too bothered that he knew about my involvement. It would keep me on my toes. The job hadn't changed.

All I had to do, still, was keep Tom out of the way while his parents got the problem sorted. Easier said than done? Possibly. I hoped not.

'There was some trouble at your parents' house,' I said eventually, breaking the silence.

'Yeah? What kind of trouble?'

'This Logan guy? Some of his men raided the place. Fortunately, your mother was able to hide herself away safely before they broke in. Then your father's security team arrived and chased them off.'

He nodded and continued fiddling with his damned phone. I might as well have told him about yesterday in Parliament.

'There was a bit of damage to the house – broken windows and doors off their hinges, and so on,' I added. 'Nothing that can't be fixed, though.'

'Right.'

His thumbs were still working away at the keyboard.

'Tom, I have to tell you this,' I said with some exasperation. 'The plan is we drop out of sight for a couple of weeks, and let your dad fix the trouble. Right?'

'Right.'

'That means we can't let anyone know where we are. If no one knows, Logan can't find us. Right?'

'Right.'

'Now I don't know who you're texting, but you'd better not tell them where we are or where we're going.'

He sighed, shook his head and gave a bitter little laugh. 'Like that, is it?'

'Yes, it is,' I said with some irritation. 'And while we're on the subject, I have to remind you that I'm at risk here, as well as you.

'You may feel your parents owe you plenty, you being a poor little rich kid and all, but I don't owe you a thing. I want you to remember that. If you put me in danger I'm going to give you hell!'

'Tough guy, eh?' he said with a sneer.

'Any time you want to find out, son, just let me know.'

The scorn and derision were inescapable, and they had got to me. I had to admit it. But I could live with that. I just didn't want him letting the world know where we were. At least he put the damned phone back in his pocket after my little outburst.

Past Guisborough we dropped down through Ormesby to the Parkway. Then we circled round the south-west edge of Middlesbrough until we hit the A19 and could start heading north into Durham. The traffic eased once we were north of Billingham, and I could give Tom some attention again.

'Who's Julie?'

His head swung round.

'She was asking about you at the house.'

'Just a girl, a friend.'

'Your girlfriend?'

'Yeah. Something like that.'

'She seemed a bit ... hazy?'

'That's her.'

'And your mum's sister was there, too. Senga?'

He nodded but didn't volunteer anything about his aunt.

'Where are we going anyway?' he asked suddenly.

'Northumberland.'

'Oh, great!' he said with a bitter little laugh.

'What's wrong with that?'

'Where do you think I've spent the last year?'

'No idea. Where?'

'Fucking Acklington – Northumberland!'

The Young Offender Centre, or whatever it was called now. I shrugged and kept going, desisting from telling him it would be different on this side of the wall.

'What are you looking at?' he asked. 'You keep watching the mirror.'

'Nothing. I'm just keeping an eye out for trouble.'

'Are you expecting any?'

I shook my head. 'Not really.'

But I wasn't sure. There had been times ever since we'd set off when I'd wondered, have I seen that vehicle before? Is this one keeping pace with us? I didn't want to be paranoid, but I didn't want any nasty surprises either.

The trouble was there were so many dark-coloured four-by-fours on the road these days, and on a major road most vehicles travel at a constant speed. Easy to imagine this one or that one was following us. Besides, realistically, how likely was it that someone could have picked us up and tailed us this far unnoticed? Not very.

Still, the possibility niggled away at me. So I slipped off the A19 and took a small road that would take us west past Trimdon Colliery and Deaf Hill, and eventually put us on the A1 Motorway.

Our speed immediately dropped to less than forty. The snow was deeper up on the Durham plateau, and the road I had taken was down to a single lane because of it. Ploughing minor roads was understandably not a high priority.

Tom's interest was aroused. 'Where are we going now?' he demanded.

'I'm cutting across to the A1. We have to do it at some point, and this is as good a route as any other.'

'So we get stuck in the fucking snow? Great thinking!'

I bit my tongue. He shook his head at the folly of us taking a snowbound minor road and returned to his smartphone. He was travelling with a total idiot.

'Let me know what the cricket score is,' I told him.

'What?'

'The third Test in India. England are playing to save the series.'

He just shook his head again. Cricket wasn't on his agenda. I wondered what was. I also wondered what he did for fun.

We reached the A1 without me seeing anything in my mirror to fuel my suspicions. I relaxed and suggested stopping at the

Durham Services place for a coffee. Tom couldn't have cared less. We stopped.

As well as coffee we had a full English, all-day breakfast. Why not? I had plenty of money from Tom's dad for expenses.

'I missed this sort of thing when I was inside,' Tom confided, betraying interest in something we were doing at last.

'What? Food?'

'*Good* food!'

I grinned. 'Welcome back, in that case.'

I wasn't sure that what we were eating qualified as *good* food, but at least the meal had brought him back to life.

'Do you need some cash?' I asked him afterwards as we headed for the exit.

He shook his head. 'I've got plenty.'

I bought a paper. Tom bought a chocolate bar. Then we headed back to the car, ready to travel on.

I started the engine and adjusted the rearview mirror just as a big pickup truck pulled up close behind. Another vehicle, a Toyota four-by-four, drew up alongside us. The door of the Toyota was flung open and banged into us.

'Hey!' Tom cried.

But I had already reacted.

We were hemmed in. The only way was forward. I slid the gear stick into first and stamped hard on the accelerator.

The car leapt forward and into a mass of shrubbery that separated one row of parking bays from the next. There might have been a concealed fence to stop us in our tracks hidden away in there. But we got lucky – there wasn't.

We burst out the other side, branches and bushes falling off the windscreen and trailing off the bonnet. I steered between two parked cars, scraping one of them with my front bumper, and turned a hard right. The tyres squealed in protest but we stayed upright. After that nothing held us back. We were away.

By the time we rejoined the motorway from the slip road we were already doing eighty. I cut between two massive trucks, ignoring the flashing lights and blaring foghorn, and took off in the fast lane.

'You OK?' I shouted.

Out of the corner of my eye I saw Tom nod.

'They were coming for us,' he said, almost in wonder. 'I saw them getting out of the vehicles.'

'Don't worry about it,' I told him.

But he was right. That was what they had been doing – coming for us. Half a dozen of them, as well.

'We're OK now,' I added. 'They have no idea where we're going. Nobody does.'

And as long as Tom kept off his bloody phone, nobody would.

'Switch your phone off, Tom.'

He nodded and did it. The message had got through to him at last.

Chapter Fourteen

WE KEPT GOING. So far as I could tell, we had lost the pursuit. Impossible to be sure while we were on the A1, with the heavy traffic around Newcastle, but it became easier when I turned onto the Jedburgh road and then, at a little place called Belsay, got onto country lanes. There was nothing behind us for miles now.

'You'll have to start navigating soon,' I said, thrusting a

road atlas at Tom.

He didn't seem very keen on the idea but he took the atlas and opened it. I told him where we were heading.

'Christ!' he said when he'd spotted our destination. 'It's bloody miles away.'

'That's the idea.'

'What will we do there?'

I hadn't really thought of that. Saving Tom's life had seemed enough of a challenge.

'We'll just get dug in, and wait for your folks to tell us the problem has been solved.'

He shook his head. 'It could be a long wait.'

'You know more than me, son, but your dad seemed pretty confident. A couple of weeks, he said.'

'And the rest!'

'You think?'

Tom shrugged. 'He should know, I suppose. He's the one that got us into this mess in the first place.'

And there was me thinking it was Tom himself who had done that. It confirmed my growing belief that I didn't know the half of it. We kept going. Twenty minutes later we passed through a big village.

'What on earth do all the people here do for a living?' Tom wondered aloud. 'Look – they've got shops and pubs, and everything!'

'It's the rural economy,' I told him loftily.

'Sheep, and stuff?'

'And forestry. Quarrying, maybe. I don't know. Where I live, fishing is pretty big, but it won't be here. Hill farming mostly, I would think.'

'Sheep, then?'

'Probably.'

We seemed to be on speaking terms now, although the conversation was pretty rudimentary. Still, I was relieved. The lad was prepared to talk to me at last. That was progress.

As we pressed on up a long valley leading into the hills, I sensed Tom's interest and enthusiasm waning. The talking stopped, apart from the occasional terse instruction to turn left or right. But finally, we were there.

It was dark by then. The two cottages were both in blackness. Without our headlights, we wouldn't even have been able to see them. No light pollution at all. Townie campaigners on that subject would have been delighted.

I left Tom in the car while I retrieved the keys from the shed where Pete had said they were kept. Then I let myself into what I'd been told was the better of the two cottages and switched on the lights.

My first impression was that it was dark, cold and damp. I walked through the place and understood why Pete had trouble letting it in winter. It was an ice-box. The ashes in the hearth had been there months, and there was no other means of heating the cottage. Condensation from my own breath hung in the air in clouds. It was utterly miserable.

We had no food either. Pete had said there would be some in the kitchen, and there was: half a dozen tins of baked beans and a couple more of tomato soup. I grimaced. We weren't that desperate.

I walked back to the car, got in and started the engine. Tom looked at me expectantly.

'We're not stopping here,' I told him. 'It's a dump. Let's get back to that village we passed through.'

'Thank Christ for that!' he said, making it sound heart-felt.

So we returned to the village we had passed through half an

hour earlier and found rooms in The Shepherd's Rest. Tom seemed hugely relieved and grateful for my decision to abandon the cottage. It had put him in a better mood. So we had a beer in the bar while we considered the evening meal menu.

'It's not bad, this place,' he said, looking round at the trappings of an ancient coaching inn.

'Better than the cottage, anyway,' I suggested.

He shuddered. Then he grinned. 'What would we have done there?'

'I'm not sure, but at least we'd have been out of sight. Abandoned and forgotten, probably. Maybe that would have been a good thing.'

We were talking again. It seemed like an opportunity to try to winkle some information out of him.

'You've had a rough year?' I suggested.

He grimaced. 'Longer than that, actually. It was all unnecessary, as well. If only my bloody father had had more sense!'

'Well, he could hardly have prevented you getting pissed, although I suppose he needn't have given you such a powerful car for a birthday present.'

'Is that what they told you it was about?' Tom shook his head. 'It goes back before that. You have no idea.'

He was right. I didn't. The situation was beginning to seem more complex with every passing moment.

'This Logan guy seems a bit special,' I suggested. 'He certainly has a lot of manpower at his disposal.'

'Yeah.' Tom paused for a moment and then added, 'He's a big operator down south somewhere.'

'London?'

'I think so.'

'A gangland boss?'

'So it seems.'

'What's he doing up here? He came, mob-handed, because of his son's death?'

Tom shook his head. 'He was here already.'

'Doing what?'

'Trying to muscle in on stuff that was nothing to do with him. Ask my dad. I don't want to talk about it.'

My perspective was changing fast. As I'd begun to suspect, there had been some sort of involvement between the Steeles and Logan even before the accident.

'But Logan's son was killed? That, at least, is true?'

Tom nodded. 'Yeah. I ran him over.'

So what did it all mean? I was even more confused. But I didn't want to milk the lad dry all in one go. So I changed the subject.

'What do you fancy to eat?'

'Steak and chips.'

'OK. Me, too. Go and place the order.'

'Put it on your room number?'

'Why not?' I said, grinning. 'For once I won't mind settling the bill.'

He got up.

'One more thing, Tom,' I said. 'Did you know Logan before all this started?'

He shook his head. 'I didn't. But my dad did, more's the pity.'

'Did that have anything to do with the accident?'

'Accident?' he said with a bitter little laugh. 'What accident?'

Chapter Fifteen

I LEFT IT there. There was plenty of time to find out more. I didn't want to push Tom hard that first evening, not when we had just started to get on a little better. Anyway, I had learned a few things already, and they were troubling me. I needed to think.

So Josh Steele had known Logan before the accident – if, indeed, accident was what it had been? I wondered how that had come about. I wondered that a lot. Josh and a London gangster? Was there an innocent explanation? I hoped so, but I wasn't confident.

And if it wasn't an accident, what was it? Tom said he had run over Logan's son, but in what circumstances? He had implied that it had been deliberate.

Tom's attitude to his father was troubling, too. There was a lot of hostility coming out of the lad. For some reason, he blamed Josh for what had happened, and for his year in custody. If he was right, the hostility was justified, but was he right?

Anne's attitude to Josh was more easily explained. She, too, blamed Josh for the trouble Tom had found – and probably for everything else as well.

Poor Josh. One way or another, things were not great in the Steele family.

I shook my head and reminded myself yet again that whatever the background story, my job was just to keep Tom safe. That was all I was being paid to do. Solving criminal mysteries – homicides even – was what Bill Peart did for a living. He could get on with it. I was going to keep things as simple and straightforward as I could.

*

Later, when I was back in my room, Bill phoned. He must have
known I'd been thinking of him. I grimaced when I saw from
the screen who it was, but I took the call.

'Hi, Bill!'

'So you are involved?'

'Say that again?'

He snorted with indignation. 'I'm going to have to drag it
out of you, am I?'

I weighed up the options. On the whole, it seemed better to
avoid antagonizing him further. We would probably need each
other again, if only to go fishing. I would struggle to get Jimmy
Mack's boat in the water single-handed. Besides, Bill wouldn't
always be able to solve crimes without my help.

'What do you want to know?'

'Everything – before I arrest you and charge you with
obstructing justice.'

I sighed. 'OK. Put the handcuffs away. Here it is. First, I
was visited yesterday morning by Mr and Mrs Steele. They
had a proposition for me.'

'Oh, boy! I can't wait to hear what it was.'

I let a silence grow between us.

'OK,' he said wearily. 'Just tell me – in your own words.'

I grinned. His need to know was greater than my need to
tell. That put me in a happy position.

'Their son, Tom, had just been released from youth custody
at a young offender centre. He'd been sent there for a drink-
driving offence.'

'And for running somebody over and killing them.'

'Well, yes. So I understand. He did run a lad over, apparently, and sadly the lad died. But Tom is a decent enough kid.
He's not a hard case or an habitual offender.'

'Spare me the character reference, Frank. I just want some

facts.'

'I'm telling you how I see him.'

'Noted.'

'Anyway, his parents were concerned for Tom because of threats they had received, threats to kill him in retaliation for the other lad's death. So they asked me to take him out of circulation and look after him while they tried to sort things out. That's what I'm doing.

'That's all I'm doing,' I added for emphasis.

'In exchange for…?'

'They're paying me a fee, if that's what you mean. Of course they are.'

'A fee of…?'

'None of your business.'

'It might be. I might make it my business.'

'That's up to you,' I said with a shrug.

He let it slide. Instead, he saw other ways of having a go at me.

'The husband and wife – and you, for that matter – didn't consider that these threats to the son might be police business?'

'Mr and Mrs Steele are very grateful for what the police have done so far,' I said tonelessly, 'but they remain very worried about the well-being of their son and decided to take additional precautions.'

He chuckled without sounding terribly amused. 'OK, Frank. I get the picture. I don't suppose you want to tell me where you've stashed the lad?'

'Nowhere at the moment. We're travelling. How are you getting on with investigating the attack on the Steeles' home?'

Another sardonic chuckle. 'They've told you, I take it, that they're at war with a man called Logan, the man whose son the Steeles' kid ran over?'

I grimaced. He was making it sound like a mafia confrontation. But perhaps that was what it was.

'I gather Logan's been attacking their business premises,' I admitted.

'He certainly has. A timber compound of theirs in South Bank went up in flames the night before last. That was the latest in a long line of such incidents. Now their home has been attacked.'

'Who is he, Bill, this Logan character?'

'I don't know much about him, but I keep hearing the "big operator down south" phrase. Boss of some sort of criminal gang. Essex-based, I gather. The death of his son seems to have brought him up here intent on wreaking vengeance.

'And now we've got a badly injured officer his thugs beat up to worry about, as well. He may not make it, I'm sorry to say.'

I grimaced. 'Sorry to hear that, Bill. But my information – my very limited information – is that Logan was here already. It wasn't the death of his son that brought him up to Teesside.'

'Is that right?' Bill said slowly. 'Now that's interesting. Did he and Steele know each other beforehand?'

'I'm told they did. But I don't know the context.'

'That's worth looking into. Thanks, Frank.'

'What do you know about Josh Steele?' I asked, eager to get something in return.

'Well, until now, he's always seemed... what's the word? Irreproachable? That's the one. A successful businessman, with a growing empire. And a pillar of the community. Lots of good works to his name.'

'Until now?'

'Well, if he knew Logan before all this kicked off, you have to wonder, don't you?'

You did, indeed.

*

Meanwhile, Tom was getting on very well. He had found a place at the pool table, where he was playing with a group of local lads. I got another pint, and sat and watched – all expenses paid. This was the life!

I soon found myself wondering about the Steele family again. It's always like that. You take on a client and before long you're deconstructing the story they told you, and trying to make better sense of it. You can't do the job you're being paid for otherwise.

What I knew now was that if I was to help Tom survive, I needed a better idea of what I was up against. I no longer believed what Josh and Anne had told me.

So Josh Steele was a successful and eminent businessman with an impressive industrial spread and a posh house. He had a smart, good-looking wife, too, even if he wasn't flavour of the month with her just now. And he had a troubled son who hadn't finished paying the price for a tragedy for which he still seemed to have been responsible.

He also had a professional criminal on his back, a man with a big reputation and a lot of resources to deploy.

Not an entirely wonderful life, after all.

The question particularly intriguing me now was the one Bill Peart had seized on: how come Steele and Logan had known each other before the death of Logan's son? There seemed no reason for it. No good reason, at least.

'Another pint, Frank?'

I looked up. 'Thanks, Tom. Game over?'

'Yeah.' He grinned and added, 'I wiped the floor with them. They're just woollybacks out here.'

'Better not let them hear you say it.'

'Oh, they're all right. Good lads, actually.'

I was pleased, and relieved. Getting on with locals his own age might make our stay here easier.

'Remember the cover story,' I told him. 'We're here for a few days convalescence as you've just come out of hospital.'

He grinned. 'Boy, you've thought of everything!'

'That's right. Every contingency. We might do a spot of fishing while we're here, you can tell them.'

'Fishing?'

He looked at me as if he was about to vomit.

'Well, we have to do something. What else is there? Walking? Bird watching?'

'I don't know. You tell me. You're the one who had the bright idea of coming here.'

'Thanks, Tom. Fishing it is, then.'

'Cod, or what?'

'Salmon or trout, Tom. It's a river they have here, not the bloody sea.'

We sat in a companionable silence for a while, watching the pool players, listening to the big wall clock sounding out the minutes and the low hum of conversation at the bar. I began to wonder if there was anything on TV.

Then Tom's phone went off while he was coming back from the gents. He answered it before I could intercept him.

'My girlfriend,' he said afterwards with a shrug, looking both uncomfortable and defiant. 'She says she's on her way here.'

Chapter Sixteen

'TELL ME IT'S not true!' I demanded.

He just shrugged again.

I sighed and rubbed my face with my hands. I couldn't believe it. After all I'd said!

'That's Julie, is it?' I asked, struggling to keep my voice neutral.

'Yeah.'

'How does she know where we are, Tom?'

'I couldn't not tell her!'

'Oh yes you could.'

'She said she's been waiting a whole year for me to get out. I had to tell her.'

'You're too soft, Tom,' I said with a weary sigh.

The bad moment had passed. My incredulity was beginning to fade. I needed to cope with the new reality.

'She stood by me,' he said stubbornly.

I nodded. 'Let's hope she doesn't get you killed.'

He gave a scornful laugh.

'What?' I said. 'You don't think Logan's bright enough to have had men watching her, ready to follow her to you?'

His expression froze as he realized the implications at last.

'Come on!' I said. 'Get your stuff together. We're leaving.'

Ten minutes later we were on the road, heading back to Pete's cottage.

'Give me your mobile,' I said.

'My phone? No way!'

'Give me it now, or I turn round and take you back to your parents' house in Marton.'

'You can't ...'

'Yes, I can.'

'My father paid you ...'

'I'll give him his money back. I can't protect you if you ignore my instructions and insist on doing stupid things I warned you about.'

'Just who the fuck do you think you are?'

I pulled over and stopped the car. I turned to look at him in the dim light from the dashboard. He looked uneasy and mad, both at the same time.

'Tom, let me spell it out again for you. Because we're together, my life is at stake, as well as yours. You might be prepared to throw your own life away, but mine isn't going with it. Do it my way, or I'm out of here.

'Now what's it to be? Are you going to hand over the phone, or do you want me to take you home to Mummy and Daddy?'

We sat still and quiet for a few moments in an atmosphere that was brittle, to say the least. Then he pulled the phone out of his pocket and handed it over without another word. He wasn't happy about it. His face was blank but he was humiliated, and I could tell that inwardly he was seething.

So what? I'd warned him more than once. And I couldn't trust him anymore.

Ten minutes up the road, he said, 'What about Julie? We should tell her.'

'Tell her what? Where we're going?'

'Let her know we've left the pub.'

I thought about it. Maybe we should. She could turn back. There was no point letting her drive all the way out here to the village.

I pulled over again and took out his phone. 'Get her. But I'll do the talking.'

He did the business and handed the phone back. It rang

twice before our call was answered.

'Tom?'

'No, it isn't Tom. But I'm with him, and I'm speaking for him.'

'Put Tom on the phone.'

It didn't sound like the dizzy young girl I'd met at the house in Marton.

'Who is this?' I asked.

'Never mind that. Just put Tom on the phone, please.'

'That's not going to happen. I'm phoning to say that we've left the place you know about, and we don't want you trying to follow us. For Tom's sake, you should turn round and go home.'

'If you don't put my nephew on the phone, my brother-in-law will skin you alive!'

Ah!

'Senga, is it?'

'Never mind who.'

'Turn round and go home, Senga. And take Julie with you. We don't want you following us. You're a danger to yourselves and to Tom.'

To quieten the stream of abuse that followed, I let Tom say a few words to shut her up. Then he told Julie he was OK. I took the phone back and switched it off.

'Will they turn back?' I asked.

He just shrugged.

That's what I thought, too. Who could tell?

'What's your aunt doing with Julie?'

'I have no idea.'

'Are they friends?'

'I really don't know. I don't know anything any more. I've been out of circulation a year, remember?'

'Well, at least you know Julie isn't on her own. So you don't need to worry about her.'

I didn't think he accepted that any more than I did myself. Realistically, there were now two potential hostages out there somewhere. I just hoped they had the sense to give up and turn back before they ran into trouble.

The cottage didn't look any better than the first time I'd seen it. Cold, dark, damp and miserable was how I summed it up, but I kept those thoughts to myself.

'First, we'll get a fire going,' I said cheerfully. 'Then we'll sit back and take stock.'

Tom took himself off to explore, while I set about getting some kindling going and then feeding the flames with well-chosen logs. Fortunately, the pile of logs beside the hearth seemed drier than the building itself. It would be a while before the fire did much to dispel the cold and the damp, but the sight and sound of it gave me a psychological boost.

'Two bedrooms,' Tom said, when he returned from his inspection of the upper floor.

I nodded.

'I'll get our stuff out of the car,' he added. 'Is it locked?'

'Yeah.'

I fished the keys out of my pocket and tossed them to him.

'It's going nicely now,' he said, looking over my shoulder.

I grinned at him. 'Ex-boy scouts all know how to make a fire.'

'Is that what you were?'

'Briefly. They chucked me out before I learned much else.'

'What for?'

'Chiefly, for starting fires in places they didn't want them.'

He liked that. He humphed with amusement, and left me to nurture the flames.

It was only when I heard the car engine start a minute or two later that I realized Tom still wasn't on my side, after all.

Chapter Seventeen

THE PHONE RANG. Blue glanced at it and pressed the button.

'Yes, Eddie?'

'The girl? She's been picked up by that other woman – the wife's sister.'

'Steele's sister-in-law?'

'Yeah – whatever. They're going somewhere. The girl had a bag.'

'What kind of bag? A shopping bag?'

'No. A leather thing.'

'Overnight bag?'

'Something like that. What do you want us to do?'

'Follow them. If they look to be heading anywhere interesting, let me know and I'll catch you up.'

Afterwards, he wondered if this might be the lead he'd been waiting for. It might be. The two women together? They were probably just going shopping, whatever Eddy thought, but ... you never could tell.

Just as well, after the fiasco at the motorway service area. The guy with the Steele kid, the PI, had been pretty good. He had to give him that. They'd had him cornered but he'd reacted quicker than them, and got away with it. God knew where they were now.

That bloody PI! He should have just shot the bastard when he had the chance. Trying to scare him off hadn't worked worth a damn. What did it matter if he was friendly with the cops? If the guy was dead, what difference did that make?

Still, with a bit of luck, the women Eddie was following might let them catch up. They needed that, a bit of luck. Logan was getting impatient, and he wasn't the only one. They had to get things moving. Otherwise heads would roll – literally.

He couldn't really give a damn about Logan but there were people he didn't want to upset, and they were not the most patient or understanding people in the world. Even he, with his record, had to be careful where they were concerned.

'Is he always like that?' Manny asked Eddie, after he hung up.

'Like what?'

'You know – pushy.'

Eddie smiled and focused on driving for a few moments.

'He's good,' he said eventually. 'The best I've ever worked with. He gets things right, and he gets them done.'

Manny pushed the cigarette lighter in and took out a packet of Marlboros. 'Too bossy for my liking.'

'He is the boss. Nobody better than Blue.'

'Yeah, well. That's another thing – his name. What's his first name?'

Eddie was stumped. He didn't know.

'It's a funny name,' Manny persisted. 'Blue? Where's that come from?'

'No idea.'

Eddie wasn't comfortable with this conversation. It felt disloyal.

'And the other day,' Manny said, 'he was talking in a foreign language – French, I think – on the phone. That's another funny thing.'

Eddie had to agree. That was strange. But then again, he

had no idea where Blue had come from, or what his history was. He was a clever bloke, though. He knew that much. Tough, as well.

'Intelligent people tend to speak more than one language,' he said loftily.

'Yeah, right,' Manny said. 'So why don't you and me?'

Eddie laughed and shook his head.

'Where are these two going?' he asked, a little worried now, as they headed ever deeper into the darkness of the countryside.

'No idea. Not shopping, anyway. We haven't seen a single light anywhere for the last half hour.'

'I'd better call Blue again.' Eddie nodded to himself, decision taken. 'Maybe this is what we've been waiting for.'

Chapter Eighteen

THERE WAS NO doubt about it – the little bastard was gone. Shit!

I stood outside the cottage and swore savagely as the tail lights of the Volvo faded and finally disappeared. This was all I needed. Whatever had possessed me to give him the bloody keys? Stupid, stupid, stupid!

I glanced up at the blackness overhead but there was no comfort there. Not a star in sight, less still a moon. If it hadn't been for the dim light escaping from the cottage window behind me, I would have been able to see nothing at all now the car was gone.

What to do?

I went back inside and took out my phone, intent on hiring a car from somewhere. No chance. There wasn't even one bar visible. No reception at all. I cursed that, too. I would have been better off in the middle of the Sahara than here in the hills of Northumberland.

There was only one thing for it. I propped a fireguard in front of the blaze I had created in the hearth, collected my still unpacked bag and blew out the candles. Bad night for it or not, I was walking.

It started to snow, and within a few minutes it was coming down heavily. Backed by an easterly wind, the snow was driving hard into my face. I pulled the hood of my jacket up. Then I got my head down and concentrated on the walking.

Visibility was next to non-existent. Even staying on the road was difficult. It was hard to see where it was in places, there was so little difference between the single-lane strip of tarmac and the ground to either side now the whole lot was covered with an inch or two of snow. I battled on at a derisory pace, often uncertain if I was walking on road or moor.

Then I bumped into something big and soft that moved, and I froze with shock. The thing snorted and twitched, knocking me sideways into something similar. That, too, moved, as did something behind me. I stood stock still, pulse racing, my senses paralysed for a moment.

Awareness returned. And my sense of smell. I realized I was in the middle of a herd of cattle spread across the road.

Not a good situation to be in. Cattle are big and heavy, and fiercely protective of their young, and I had disturbed them. They had been standing quietly, stoically, packed close together for defence against wind and snow. Now they were restless, sensing my intrusion but not knowing what or where I was. If I stirred them into moving en masse, they would make mush of me.

I edged sideways gingerly, scarcely daring to breathe. A blast of hot, moist air in my face told me I was close to one end or the other of something big. I froze again.

The thing lurched away, creating a small space. I moved on, heart pounding. I couldn't see a thing. There was just blackness before my eyes, and a swirling, hissing fusillade of sharp particles driving into my face.

At last I reached a point where my outstretched left hand felt nothing but space. I kept going and with relief found I was free of the herd at last. I stumbled into a ditch, and icy water gurgled and soaked my lower legs. Grimly, I scrambled out and pressed on until I sensed the herd was well behind me and I could reclaim the road.

Soon after that the snow eased and I was able to make better progress. But I had a long way to go still. Ten miles from the cottage to the village? I reckoned I had encountered the cattle three or four miles along the road. At least six to go, then. Nothing for it but to bash on.

Nearly three hours after setting out, I saw my first light. Just the one, from an isolated farmhouse, but it gave me hope. Another twenty minutes and I was entering the outskirts of the village. I was pretty knackered by then but adrenaline kept me going all the way to the pub where Tom and I had briefly set down our bags. The Volvo was parked right outside. I scowled and headed for the entrance.

Things were quiet inside. A couple of middle-aged working men in hi-vis jackets occupied high stools at the bar. Two young women I recognized sat at a table nursing drinks. That was it. There was no one else. I made straight for the women.

'Where is he?'

Senga looked up at me uncertainly and then peered hard. 'Oh, it's you! The great bodyguard and private detective.'

'Where's Tom?'

She shrugged. Julie, beside her, burst into tears.

'Is he upstairs?' I asked, leaning down towards Senga, feeling very confrontational.

She swept her hair out of the way. Then I saw the bruising on her face and the eye that was swollen nearly shut. I glanced sideways at Julie, and saw a girl who was in a state of near collapse. Something bad had happened here.

I shook more snow off my jacket and sat down.

'What happened?'

'They took him,' Senga said in a monotone.

'Who did? Logan's people?'

She nodded. 'I tried to stop them, but ...'

But they had flattened her, obviously. Thrown her aside like a crumpled crisp packet.

'How did it happen, and how long ago?'

'There were three or four of them. They just came up on us, grabbed Tom, smacked me out of the way, and bundled him into a car. Then they took off.'

'How long ago?' I repeated.

'An hour?' She shrugged. 'I don't really know.'

Then she wheeled round on me as if telling the tale had released her from the paralysis of shock. 'You were supposed to prevent this!' she hissed. 'You were paid a lot of money to protect Tom.'

'Short of putting him in handcuffs and leg-irons, I did what I could,' I assured her. 'He stole the car and took off when I wasn't looking. I've had a ten-mile walk through a blizzard just to get here.'

She looked unconvinced. To hell with her!

'Anyway,' I added, 'it was you two that led Logan here. If you'd stayed at home, or gone back, like I told you, they'd have had no idea where Tom was.'

She glared at me then as if she wanted to cut my throat. I held her gaze for a long moment. Then I said, 'So they got Tom. Has anybody done anything about it?'

'The landlord phoned the police,' Senga said. 'That's all that's happened.'

She seemed fatalistic about it, as if she didn't expect anything to come of that.

'What did they say?'

'Not much. They took details, but they can't do anything right now – they can't get here because of the snow. I shouldn't have blamed you,' she added wearily, motioning towards Julie. 'We're just exhausted.'

'I can see that. Are you booked in here?'

'We are now.'

'Why don't you get Julie to bed? Give her some paracetamol and a hot drink.'

Senga looked at me as if I wasn't right in the head.

'The girl's in shock,' I said patiently. 'She needs to sleep.'

That got through to her. She nodded and began to move.

'Do you need me to help you get her upstairs?'

'No. We'll manage. We can both still walk, thank you very much!'

I stood up and took off my coat. I was beginning to warm up.

'What are you going to do?' Senga asked.

'I'm going to have a word with the landlord first, and then with the police.'

'Are you going to let Josh and Anne know?'

'Not yet. Not until the situation is clearer.'

She nodded and began to manoeuvre Julie towards the

exit from the bar. I was thinking Senga seemed more reasonable now. That was a relief. One woman in an angry rage and
another in a state of collapse would have been more than I
could cope with.

The landlord was in a little cubby hole of an office behind the
bar. He was just putting the phone down when I knocked on
the door.

'Can I help you?' he asked with a weary smile.

'I'm a friend of the lad that just got abducted. Where do
things stand?'

He looked at me with more interest. 'I've just been on to the
police again. They say they won't be able to get here for a while
because the snow's too deep over Alnwick Moor. Six-foot drifts,
apparently. They'll have to wait for a plough to make a way
through.'

'Is that the only way in and out of the village?'

'Well, put it this way. If the main road to Alnwick is
closed, there's no chance at all of any of the alternatives being
passable.'

I grimaced. That didn't sound good.

'Did anybody manage to get the licence plate number of the
car Tom was taken off in?'

'Tom? Oh, yes. Tom Steele, isn't it? One of the women got the
number. I've passed it on to the police.'

I wondered if they might be able to spot the car and intercept it. Maybe. It was possible, although the weather wasn't
going to help. I couldn't believe visibility would be much better
than it was here anywhere in the region.

'How long has the Alnwick road been closed?'

He shrugged. 'A couple of hours? I don't really know.'

So Logan's gang might not have got clean away, I thought.

They could be stuck in a snowdrift on the moor, freezing to bloody death. It was a comforting thought. Pity about poor Tom, of course, but he deserved to be there with them. He was the one who had created this mess. He couldn't blame his father for this one.

But it really wasn't a laughing matter. Logan had Tom. What now?

If he'd just wanted him dead, Tom could be gone already. I decided to work on the assumption that he was still alive.

I phoned the police. They told me the main road out of the village had been closed for a couple of hours, as the landlord had suspected. When I mentioned the abduction, and how urgent the situation was, the officer I spoke to retreated into defensive mode.

'We're doing the best we can,' he told me. 'There have been no reports of a vehicle with the licence plate we were given.'

'What do you know about the vehicle?'

'All I can tell you, *sir,* is that this is a police matter – and it's in hand.'

Great. I swallowed the retort that came instantly to mind. Then I gave him my name and phone number, and asked to be kept informed.

'Your interest is?'

'I'm a friend of the family.'

He wasn't impressed. We didn't get any further. I couldn't blame him. He was right. It was police business. But it was also family business – and my business.

So I called Josh, and had a difficult conversation with him.

'All I can tell you for sure, Josh, is that Tom left the cottage where we were going to be staying and drove into a village a few miles away. That's where Logan's people picked him up.'

'Jesus Christ, Frank! How the hell did you let that happen?'

'I don't feel good about it, Josh. I can tell you that. But Tom fooled me. I thought we were on the same side. Evidently, we weren't. He took the car keys and beat it, leaving me with a ten-mile hike through a blizzard to the nearest village. That's where Logan's people caught him.'

'So it's his fault, is it? That's what you're saying? It's all my son's fault?'

I said nothing to that.

'And how did Logan find where you were, anyway?' Josh demanded angrily.

'It wasn't difficult. Despite my repeated warnings and threats – and despite my confiscating his phone – Tom found a way of contacting his girlfriend and letting her know where he was.'

There was a big sigh at the other end then. Josh was starting to get the picture. 'Tom's got more than one phone,' he said in a resigned tone.

'So I've realized.'

'Then what?' he added. 'Julie is on his side for crissake! She wouldn't have told anyone where Tom was.'

'She didn't have to. She just came to visit him, despite me telling her not to. Guess who was waiting for that to happen? Guess who followed her all the way here?'

'Oh, shit!'

'There's more you need to know.'

'What?'

'Julie didn't come alone. She came with Anne's sister.'

'Senga? What the hell for?'

'I don't know. You'll have to ask her. But they're both here now.'

Josh took a moment to digest that. Then he said, 'What about Tom? Where does all this leave him?'

'I don't know, Josh. I'm just guessing. But I don't think they'll have done anything to him. If they'd just wanted him dead, they would have shot him on the spot, not kidnapped him.

'Maybe they plan to use him as a hostage. I don't know. Is there anything else Logan wants from you? I understand you've had some dealings with him?'

Josh didn't answer that. Instead, he said, 'So where have they taken him?'

'Who knows? We're snowed in here and the police say they won't be able to reach us until the snow ploughs break through, which I would guess will be sometime tomorrow. If Logan's people got out before the road was closed, the police have a licence plate to watch for. That's as much as I know.'

'What if they didn't get out before the road was shut?'

'In that case,' I said, 'they're stuck in a snowdrift somewhere between here and Alnwick.'

Chapter Nineteen

ALTHOUGH I'D KEPT calm talking to Josh, my insides were in turmoil. Tom was in big trouble. I could soothe his father all I liked, but that was the reality. There wasn't much I could do to help him now either. The fact that Tom himself had engineered this situation didn't make me feel any better about it.

There was certainly nothing more I could do from the warmth and comfort of a modernized eighteenth-century coaching inn. So I put my coat back on and took the spare set of car keys out of my bag. Then I went to see if I could start the Volvo.

It started fine. In a howling gale I dusted the snow off the windscreen and side windows, got in and turned the car round. By then, the windows were covered again. The snow was slanting down harder than ever, and the headlights scarcely penetrated the billowing sheets. Visibility was little more than non-existent. It was bitterly cold, as well.

After a brief hesitation I set off in first gear, wondering how far I would get before the snow brought the car to a halt. Here, it was six or seven inches deep, which was just about negotiable, but I suspected it wouldn't be long before I had to turn back. I just wanted to make sure Logan's car wasn't stuck somewhere close to the village.

After a couple of hundred yards I rounded a bend and ran into a drift of snow that was nearly as high as the car itself. I stopped and peered ahead aghast. A ferocious wind was driving the snow like fast-flowing water down the lower slopes of the moor and over the road. The drift was wider than I could see, and I wasn't even on the moor yet.

There was nothing to be done. I reversed back the way I had come, while I still could. Where the road was sheltered by the first of the buildings in the village, I turned round and drove back a little way until I could park on some open ground just before I reached the pub.

I collected one or two things from the car and made my way back to the pub, head down against the wind, trudging through snow that was over the tops of my boots now. It was going to be a difficult night for a lot of people, Tom amongst them – assuming he was still alive.

The landlord was in his little office. He was talking to the barmaid, who was understandably anxious to close down and get away home for the night. I gathered she lived nearby in the village, which was just as well given the conditions.

'Yes, off you go, Amy. There's no point keeping you here any longer. It's not as if we're likely to get any more customers tonight.'

Amy looked relieved. She thanked him, gave me a quick smile and went hunting for her coat.

The landlord looked up at me and said with surprise, 'Have you been out?'

I nodded and dusted some of the fresh snow off my jacket. 'I didn't get far, though.'

'What's it like?'

'You wouldn't believe it.'

'Oh, I would!' he said, chuckling. 'I've lived here all my life. A bit of snow's not going to surprise me.'

'That's good to hear. But you might want to wait a while before closing up for the night.'

He looked at me suspiciously.

'We've got a problem,' I said.

'*We* have, have we?'

'Two, actually,' I said, nodding. 'Think about it.'

He realized I was serious. Sensible man, he just sat there, waiting for me to continue.

'First, I've just driven up the road a couple of hundred yards. I got stopped by a drift that Hannibal and his elephants wouldn't have got through, and I hadn't even reached the moor. The gang that abducted Tom would have got a lot further than me because they set off earlier, but I doubt if they got all the way through. They'll have been stopped somewhere higher up, probably.'

'By Pit Cottage, I would think,' the landlord said, thinking about it. 'That's the highest point on the moor.'

I nodded, and wished I knew the local topography. That would have come in handy. I'd have to see if I could get hold of a map.

'They'll probably just sit there in the car for a while, waiting for the snow to stop, but it'll soon get too cold for that. Eventually, they'll set off to walk back here, because it's the only place they know about.

'When they get here, my guess is they'll make for the pub. If you've put out the lights and locked the door, they'll just force their way in and help themselves. Anyone wanting to survive on a night like this would be entitled to do the same.'

He grimaced and said, 'So what do you suggest I do? Stay open and offer them hospitality? Pretend nothing has happened?'

'It might be your best plan. There's no police presence here, is there?'

He shook his head and said, 'To hell with that! I'll get some of the local lads. We'll soon see these buggers off.'

'They're tough people.'

'Not like the folk around here, you mean? You haven't seen my neighbours!'

'This lot will almost certainly be armed.'

'So what? A lot of us have shotguns.'

Shotguns? I shook my head and pulled a face.

'What's wrong with that?'

'Shotguns wouldn't do it,' I told him. 'If you take them on, you'll end up with some orphans and widows in the village, as well as having your pub smashed up. These are serious criminals. Big time. They'll be armed with weapons a lot more potent than shotguns, and they're used to shooting people with them.'

I paused to let that sink in and then added, 'It would be better to offer them hospitality, and wait for the police to arrive.'

He was thinking about it now, weighing up what I'd said.

'You said there were two problems,' he queried. 'What's the other one?'

'The women staying here. If and when the gang come back, they'll look for those women. They know they're associated with Tom Steele. They probably know who they are. So they're vulnerable. Potential hostages, if nothing else. We need to move them.'

'*We* need to move them?' he repeated slowly. He looked at me for a moment and shook his head. 'Since when did I become responsible for them?'

'Since you gave them rooms in your hotel. At least since then.'

He sighed. 'Aye, you're right,' he admitted. 'This is turning out to be quite a night, isn't it? Who did you say you were, by the way?'

'Frank Doy. I'm a security consultant and private investigator, retained by his family to protect Tom Steele.'

'James Cummings, landlord.'

Belatedly, perhaps, we shook hands. He seemed to have accepted at last that we were on the same side. Thankfully, he didn't offer a snide comment on how well I seemed to have done so far in looking after Tom.

'James, we need to get the ladies out of here. If the gang ask where they are, just say they left an hour or two ago. You have no idea where they were going. They never said.'

'So we need to move them somewhere,' he said briskly, straightening up in his chair.

'Don't ask me where,' I told him. 'I haven't a clue.'

'I can help there. We've got a little cottage, a holiday let, that's empty at the moment.'

'In the village?'

He nodded.

'That sounds ideal. I'll go and get them.'

'Rooms two and three!'

Senga was in Julie's room. She wasn't pleased to see me.

'What do you want?'

'A word, if you don't mind.'

She stepped out into the corridor and gently closed the door behind her.

'Is she asleep?' I asked.

She nodded.

'We're going to have to wake her up.'

'I don't think so,' she said with a scornful chuckle.

So I explained the situation. After a moment's thought, she seemed to accept it.

'There's just one problem,' she said. 'Julie won't be able to walk now. I gave her a sleeping pill, a strong one. So we might have to carry her.'

'Let's hope it's not far, then,' I said grimly. 'I've had about enough for one night.'

Chapter Twenty

IT WASN'T FAR to the cottage. Between us, we managed to get Julie there safely. James led the way and stayed to show us how things worked. Then he returned to the hotel, preparing himself for a stressful night. He had my sympathy.

'If they do turn up,' I told him, 'just behave normally. They're new guests who got caught by the snow. Don't question or provoke them, and don't let them know that you're aware of what went on earlier.'

'That's not going to be easy.'

'Do it, James! Just do it.'

'What if it all goes pear-shaped?'

'Walk away. Leave. Let them get on with it.'

He didn't think much of that advice, but what alternative would he have? I didn't want him or any of his neighbours getting themselves badly beaten or killed, not even for Tom – especially for Tom!

It was different for me. I had signed on to protect the lad, and I wasn't going to renege on that commitment now. Professional pride, personal honour, me being stubborn? All of that, and more. He was a young kid who might be bolshy, and at times downright unpleasant with it, but he didn't deserve what had happened to him.

It was a two-bedroom cottage, with a big living room and a kitchen downstairs. I helped Senga get Julie onto one of the beds upstairs, and then left them to it. Julie hadn't really woken up.

'Those pills must be strong,' I remarked before I left.

Senga nodded.

'Whose are they? Yours or hers?'

'Mine.'

So Julie wouldn't be used to them. A minimum dose had probably been enough.

'You should get some sleep, as well,' I suggested. 'Use the other bedroom. I won't need it.'

'What are you going to do?'

I motioned towards the window in the living room, which gave a good view of the main street. 'I'll be in here. I want to know if and when they come back.'

I sat in the near dark, with just a few pinpricks of light behind me from the television, the cooker and other electrical equipment on standby. I didn't need more. Where I did need plenty of light was just outside the village pub. Fortunately, James had kept his illuminated sign and entrance lights ablaze. So I wouldn't miss Logan's men, if they did appear.

It was cold in the cottage, but nothing like Pete's holiday let up the valley had been. This house had central heating, which James had switched on before he left. Already the air felt different. I was quite comfortable stationed in front of the window overlooking the street. More importantly, as an observer I had a prime position.

I watched the snow slanting down, sometimes in sheets, sometimes in energetic, swirling squalls as the wind lost track of what it was supposed to be doing and went haywire for minutes on end. Much of the time I had only a murky view through the snow to the pub's entrance, but I kept my eyes fastened on it and I saw no one go in or out.

All the time, the snow in the street was piling up. A foot now? Something like that. Deeper in places, where the howling wind had driven it up against the walls of a house or an obstruction like the public phone box. The way things were going, it might be next spring, not tomorrow, before the snow ploughs made their breakthrough.

It was noisy outside but the cottage was noisy, too, surprisingly so. The heating system was going full blast to drive the chill out of the building. The boiler was giving off a purposeful roar and the pipes carrying heated water groaned and rattled as it surged its way around the circuit. Walls creaked and floorboards gave out alarming cracks as the warmth started to get to them. A tap ran in the bathroom. A toilet flushed. A bedroom door snapped shut. Senga, presumably. Keeping vigil, or getting ready for bed.

I did wonder about her. Julie was a straightforward case of a distraught young girl loyally trying to keep up with her boyfriend, determined enough but simply unable to cope with a situation she couldn't really comprehend. Senga was different. Senga was ... what?

Well, she was Anne's sister, apparently. I didn't remember her from earlier times, and couldn't recall ever even hearing of her, but I was prepared to accept that that was what she was. Probably two or three years younger than Anne, which would explain why she wasn't in my memory bank. Other people's younger sisters and brothers don't usually figure in your thoughts very much when you're eighteen or nineteen.

Initially hostile to me, she seemed to have mellowed and calmed down a bit. Perhaps reality had set in, and she had realized I was the only person around here capable of helping the Steele family.

Then there was her support for Tom. It wasn't the lad's mother that had followed him here; it was his aunt. Admittedly, she had come in tandem with his girlfriend, but it still spoke of a high level of commitment. She must be very fond of him, or very right-minded. Either way, it was unusual.

She seemed to be tough, as well, and I was glad of that. Over the next few hours she might well be called on to prove it.

Otherwise, I knew nothing about her. She was a complete stranger, and a mystery. But I knew someone who might know more than me, and I had time to fill while I waited for something to happen.

'Hi, Jac! It's Frank here. How are you?'

'Well, hello, Frank! What a surprise. I'm just fine, thank

you. How about yourself?'

Jac Picknett, who at one time had looked like being the love of my life, but who hadn't fancied how I lived. Still good friends, though.

'I'm good, Jac. Snowed in at the moment, but nothing is spoiling.'

'Snowed in? Risky Point is so like that, isn't it?' she said with an audible shiver and the little laugh I remembered so well. 'Just a teeny little bit remote and exposed to the elements.'

Ha, ha! I decided not to disclose my current whereabouts. That wasn't why I'd called her.

'Jac, I owe you a thank-you, and a bunch of flowers, for putting some business my way.'

'You do?' she said suspiciously. 'How did that come about?'

'Anne Fenwick. Remember her? Now Anne Steele, of course, as she has been for many years.'

'Oh, yes! Dear Anne. So she did contact you, did she? I remember once mentioning you to her.'

'Not recently, then?'

'No, no. Some time ago.'

'Well, she and her husband Josh have discovered a need for my services. Them and Anne's sister. Remember her? I never knew Anne had a sister.'

'Oh, Senga! Of course I remember her. She and I were contemporaries at college. A wild child. No doubt she is still.'

'Wild?'

'I'm being unfair. We all lived in a bit of a frenzy while we were at college, even those who, like Senga, had a baby to take care of. I was thinking more of her artwork.'

'Not serene and tranquil, I take it?'

Jac laughed. 'Far from it! Some of her paintings … Dreadful, terrifying stuff.'

That was interesting. Senga, the one-time art student, one of the wild ones. I could imagine that somehow.

'I saw Senga not long ago, actually,' Jac added. 'She had a handsome Frenchman in tow, a good bit older than her. So perhaps she has settled down now.'

'No,' I told her. 'I don't believe she has. She doesn't strike me as the family sort.'

Just as I was wondering where Senga and child lived, with or without said Frenchman, Jac added something else interesting.

'She didn't keep the child, of course.'

'No?'

'Oh, no. How could she? That would have cramped her style too much, as we used to say. Besides, she was far too young to have a baby.'

Senga in a nutshell, eh? Perhaps she was taking her role as an aunt more seriously than she had taken her role as a mother.

But it didn't sound as if she and Jac had ever been great pals.

Chapter Twenty-One

I TIRED OF watching the snow come down and phoned Bill Peart. Maybe he could help.

'What are you up to?' he demanded.

'The same old thing. You?'

'I'm off duty. So I'm sitting here watching the football on the telly.'

'You haven't taken the wife for a night out, then?'

'She's round at the church, doing something meaningless to me.'

'Like helping someone, you mean?'

'Oh, boy! That's good, coming from you.'

I flipped a mental switch. Otherwise we could have gone on all night like that.

'I'm out in the wilds of Northumberland, Bill. And snowed in. We've got a blizzard here.'

'Oh? Not again!'

'What?'

'Middlesbrough. They just conceded another goal. Much more of this and I'm switching it off. My nerves are in tatters.'

I shook my head and resumed the story.

'I brought the Steeles' lad here to get him away from trouble, and guess what?'

'Go on. I'm listening.'

'He pinched the car keys and took off, trying to get back to mainstream life. He contacted his girlfriend and told her where he was, despite everything I'd told him. And she came running, bringing his aunt with her – and Logan not far behind!'

'Party time, eh?'

'That's about right. By the time I caught up with them, Logan's gang had arrived on the scene and abducted the lad. They took off in a hurry but there's a good chance they won't have been able to get far through the snow. So I'm sitting here waiting to see if they come back.'

The sigh at the other end suggested he was reluctantly tuning into what I was telling him.

'Presumably my colleagues on the Northumbria Force know all this?'

'Some of it. But at present they can't get in here anymore

than we can get out. They were given the number of the car Tom Steele was taken off in, but I doubt that will do any good.'

'No, probably not. If Logan's gang get through the snow, they'll swap vehicles. They'll have another one waiting somewhere. Either that or they'll just take one.'

'That's what I think.'

There was a lull in the conversation. Then Bill said, 'So why did you call me? What do you want?'

'I just thought you might be interested, given that you're working on the attack on the Steeles' home in Marton.'

'And?'

'Well, I wondered if you might be able to find out how the hunt for Logan's vehicle is going. Tap into your professional network, perhaps?'

'And then tell you? Like it isn't confidential police business?'

'Well … I'm seriously worried about the lad, Bill. I don't want him to end up dead.'

'There is that, I suppose,' he agreed reluctantly. 'Right. I'll look into it.'

That was that. Suddenly the phone was dead.

I grimaced and stared at the phone. I really wished he wouldn't do that. What's wrong with being polite, and offering a bit of courtesy? What does it cost to say 'Goodbye!' or 'Have a nice day!' Something normal like that – like he does when he wants something from me.

'Who was that on the phone?'

'A friend,' I said, looking over my shoulder to see Senga approaching. I hadn't heard her come into the room.

'At a time like this?'

'He's a cop on the Cleveland Force. He might come in useful.'

'Josh doesn't want police involvement, Frank. He told you that.'

'He's already got it. They turned up at the house, remember? Besides, what about the local police up here? They're involved now.'

'They don't count.'

I smiled wryly to myself in the dark, and wondered about that. I wondered why the Northumbria police didn't count, and I wondered why the Steeles didn't want police involvement anyway.

'Has Josh had a bad experience with the cops?' I murmured.

'He doesn't think they can do any good. He thinks they might make a bad situation worse.'

'So he'd rather handle it on his own?'

She didn't respond.

'Well, he's not doing great so far. Let's hope he's proved right in the long run.'

She was very close to me now. I could smell her scent and feel the heat from her body. She was fast becoming a serious distraction.

'Has anything happened?' she asked quietly.

'Not yet. And I'm going wonky-eyed staring at the snow.'

'Want me to take over for a bit?'

'Later, maybe. Not just yet. I thought you were going to get some sleep?'

I felt her head shake. 'I would have had to take a couple of sleeping tablets, and I'm not ready to do that. You don't want two of us in a coma.'

'Julie still out for the count?'

'Yes. She will be for a good while yet.'

I wondered why Senga needed sleeping tablets. Perhaps she led a stressful life. Good training for what we'd got here.

We were both quiet for a little while, listening to the wind and watching the swirling snow. Then she asked me if I would like a coffee.

'That's an excellent idea.'

I was getting used to this different, friendlier version of Senga, and I was rather glad the first one was taking time out.

She returned a few minutes later with two mugs of coffee and we continued sitting there in a companionable silence, side by side, waiting.

'How come you're involved in all this?' I asked after a while.

'Why shouldn't I be? I'm Tom's aunt.'

'Yes, but it's you here, not his mother.'

'Anne is very busy.' She shrugged and added, 'I came with Julie.'

'Did she ask you?'

'Sort of.'

She wasn't going to volunteer much. I could see that. Even so, perhaps Julie found Senga more sympathetic than Anne, who had seemed scarcely able to stand her.

I tried to lighten the mood. 'To be perfectly honest,' I told her, 'I'm not entirely sure how I came to be involved myself.'

'It's very simple. I recommended you.'

'Really? Do you know me?'

'I have a friend who does.'

'And who's that?'

'Jac Picknett.'

'Jac, eh?'

She nodded. 'I exhibit very occasionally in her gallery.'

'You're an artist?'

'My! You're quick.'

Not really. Not at all, in fact. I was still wondering which sister was telling the truth about contacting me. I was also still wondering who had left the footprints around my cottage.

'What's that?' Senga said, pointing.

I strained to see what she had spotted. Then the veil of snow thinned for a moment and I saw them, too. Several figures were just entering the pub.

'Is it them?' she whispered. 'It is, isn't it? What are we going to do, Frank?'

'Nothing,' I said firmly.

'But if it's Tom...'

'We're going to wait and see,' I said even more firmly. 'No point rushing in.'

Chapter Twenty-Two

THE SNOW WAS driving in so thick and hard that it was hard to see where they were, or where they were going. But Blue caught a glimpse of something and stopped suddenly.

'What's up?' Eddie croaked, head down, bumping into him. 'What have you stopped for?'

'We're there.'

'Where? I can't see a fucking thing.'

'There's lights in front of us. See them?'

They stood and peered through the swirling snow, shielding their eyes with their hands.

'You're right,' Eddie said. 'I can see them now.'

'See what?' Big Cyril panted, trudging through the snow to catch them up.

'The village,' Blue said. 'We've reached it.'

'Thank Christ for that!' Manny gasped.

Manny and Cyril were dragging and pushing Tom Steele, who was in a state of near collapse. They all stood for a few moments, heads down, catching their breath and resting aching limbs.

'Fucking snow!' Manny said bitterly. 'I've had enough of it.'

The others ignored the comment but after the last couple of hours they knew how Manny felt. They had all done their share of bitching along the way. But they were here now, Blue thought. All that pain would soon be behind them.

'What now?' Eddie asked, turning to Blue.

'We'll head for that pub where we picked the kid up.'

'It won't be open.'

'If it isn't, we'll open it.'

'Someone might recognize us.'

'So what? What are they going to do? Call the cops?' Blue chuckled. 'How are they going to get here?'

Blue right again, Eddie thought with a reluctant smile.

Still chuckling, Blue led the way into the village.

The pub's lights were still on, which was promising as well as surprising. Blue had no idea what time it was, but late seemed a pretty fair assumption.

'What about him?' Big Cyril said with a nod towards Tom as they neared the entrance to The Shepherd's Rest. 'Knock him off and dump him?'

'If we were going to do that, we'd have done it a long time ago. We'll take him inside with us. I'm not too sure what Logan wants us to do with him now.'

Another consideration for Blue was that they were probably stuck here for a while. It wouldn't make sense to do anything to the kid until they were well out of it. No point courting trouble.

He turned and studied Tom in the light from the lamp over the entrance to the pub. He was about to warn him to keep his mouth shut but it seemed unnecessary. Not only could the kid not walk unsupported, but his eyes were shut as well as his mouth.

'Young kids!' Manny said with disgust. 'They've got no stamina these days. They spend too much time playing them fucking computer games.'

'I can't have any stamina either,' Eddie confided. 'I'm knackered, as well – and I'm frozen and starving!'

'You're too little, Eddie,' Big Cyril said cheerfully. 'I keep telling you. You should eat more.'

'I would be like you then, wouldn't I? A big, bloated—'

'Knock it off!' Blue snapped. 'We'll go inside now, refugees from the snow. Keep the kid well away from anybody in there.'

The bar was the only room with lights on. It seemed to be deserted.

'Anybody home?' Blue shouted.

James appeared after a few moments. 'Gentlemen! Can I help you?'

Blue walked over to him.

'You all look about done in,' James said, running his eyes over the group. 'What happened? Car get stuck?'

'We've had to walk a few miles,' Blue conceded, nodding and blowing on his hands. 'We had to abandon the car. I've never seen snow like it.'

'Oh, it can drift fast and deep up there on the moor,' James said. 'This is wild Northumberland.'

'Good thing you're still open.'

'It is. At times like this I keep the door open – just in case.'

'Good thing for you, I meant,' Blue said, a grim expression on his face. 'Saved us breaking the door down.'

'So what can I do for you?' James asked with an uneasy smile. 'You'll be wanting to stay the night, I assume?'

'Yeah. We don't have much choice. Have you got any spare rooms?'

'Twenty-three, at the last count. You're in luck.'

The expression on Blue's face told James luck didn't come into it. One way or another, he would have had to accommodate the new arrivals. Other guests would have been thrown out into the snow, if necessary.

'We'll take three rooms. Many other guests?'

'None at all. Everyone else either got away in time or didn't bother coming in the first place.'

'There were a couple of women here when we looked in earlier. What about them?'

'Oh, they left hours ago. They'll have got well away before the road was blocked.'

Maybe, Blue thought. Maybe not.

James took three numbered keys from a board behind the bar.

'The rooms are on the first floor. I'll let you find your own way up there. There's only me here tonight, and I'd better hang around in case anybody else comes in.'

Blue nodded and took the keys. 'We'll want something to eat.'

'I can't offer you much, I'm afraid. The kitchen's closed till breakfast time. There's no staff here. But I could make a few sandwiches, if that would do you?'

'Coffee, as well.'

'And coffee,' James assured him. 'There's also coffee- and tea-making facilities in the rooms. The young lad there looks as if he needs something hot.'

Blue turned and looked at Tom, who was slumped on a bench seat, propped up by Manny and Big Cyril. 'He'll be all right. He's just a bit tired and cold.'

'I can see that.'

'Whisky would do it!' Big Cyril called.

James smiled dutifully. 'If that's what you'd like.'

'Not now,' Blue said quickly. 'We'll find the rooms first.'

'They're here,' James said quietly into the phone. 'Four of them, plus the young lad.'

Frank was relieved. Thank God for that! Although he'd seen the group arrive, he hadn't been able to tell if Tom was with them.

'How is the boy?'

'Frozen and exhausted, from the looks of him.'

'Have they knocked him about?'

'Hard to tell. I didn't see him earlier. I've given them three rooms on the first floor, by the way, and left them to get on with it.'

'Well done.'

'So what happens now?'

'Just treat them like normal guests. And be careful what you say. No upsets.'

Blue had one room to himself. The others shared. On a rota basis, there would always be one of them in a room with Tom.

Blue phoned Logan.

'No names!' Logan snapped as soon as he answered the phone.

'None at all,' Blue agreed with a sigh and a shake of the head.

'You're calling me on your bloody mobile? What's the matter with you?'

'Where we are the landline's down, knocked out by the snow.'

'Where the hell's that? No! Don't tell me. I don't want to

know. What's going on?'

'We've got him. That's why I'm phoning. Do we bring him back, or … It's up to you.'

After a long pause, Logan said, 'Bring him back. We can use him.'

'Are you sure?'

'Bring him back.'

'It'll take us a while. Nothing's going to move around here until they get a snow plough through. God knows when that will be.'

Logan switched off.

Annoyed, Blue stared at the dead phone in his hand for a moment. The man had no fucking respect! But one day soon it would be different. One day soon Logan would be grovelling, and stammering apologies. That day couldn't come soon enough.

So far as he was concerned, Logan's assets were not worth all the hassle. It would have been better to do it all himself. But he didn't make these decisions. He just followed orders.

Chapter Twenty-Three

AT LEAST TOM was alive still. That had been my main worry. It would have been easy for them to have put a bullet in his head. Or just abandon him – the snow would soon have done the job for them. So perhaps they didn't really want him dead, after all? Not yet, at least.

I switched the phone off and turned to Senga.

'It is them, and they've got Tom.'

'So I gathered. How is he?'

I shrugged. 'James says he's cold and tired, but nothing more.'

She pulled a chair up and sat down close to me. 'What now?' she asked.

'I'm puzzled. They could have got rid of Tom by now. Why haven't they?'

'Killed him, you mean?'

'You prefer a spade to be called a spade, do you?'

I don't think she smiled. Neither did I. It wasn't funny really.

'Killing Tom in revenge was what I understood Logan wanted,' I continued. 'So why haven't they done it? They wouldn't even have had to waste a bullet. They could have just abandoned him, and let the weather do the rest. It wouldn't have taken long in these temperatures.'

I felt, rather than saw, Senga shake her head. 'You still don't understand, do you? You just don't get it.'

'Understand what?'

'It's true Logan did threaten to take Tom's life, but that's not what he really wants.'

'Oh? That's news to me. It's not what Josh and your sister said when I took the job.' I stared hard at her. 'So what is he after?'

'Josh's business, or a large part of it.'

'The motor dealership?'

She shook her head again. 'The main business.'

'And what's that?'

She didn't say anything for a moment, probably mulling over what she could safely tell me.

'Come on!' I urged. 'It's a bit late to be keeping things from me now. And I don't mind telling you I'm getting pretty sick of being kept in the dark.'

'Did you go to the compound where they keep the cars?' she asked eventually.

'I did, yes.'

'What else did you see there, besides cars?'

I shrugged. 'Offices, mechanics, big sheds, high-security fencing – Gerald ...'

'What else?' she said impatiently.

I was in no mood for games. I was getting pretty pissed off with the whole Steele family. They'd got me here under false pretences, it seemed. I was about ready to walk out on the whole damned lot of them, Tom and Senga included. Well, I would have been if it hadn't been for all that bloody snow.

'You tell me,' I suggested with remarkable restraint.

'Was there just cars there?'

'There was a lot of industrial equipment, as well, if that's what you mean. Diggers and wagons, and that sort of thing.'

'What else?'

I sighed wearily. 'Hell, I don't know! Big sheds, a jetty, the river—'

'And?' she interrupted.

Then I got it at last.

'The ship?'

'The ship,' she confirmed with satisfaction. 'And what do ships do?'

Now we were getting somewhere.

'Carry things across the sea. Import-export?'

'Export only, in this case.'

'Export?' I repeated thoughtfully, my brain beginning to fill in the gaps in my knowledge.

My phone went off just then, putting a stop to the exercise.

'Yes, James?'

'My sandwiches weren't good enough for them. They wanted bacon and eggs. I told them I have no kitchen staff overnight, but that wasn't good enough for them either. So I told them just to get on with it themselves, which is what they're doing right now.'

'Do you get a discount if you do your own cooking?'

'Very funny! Now, what do you need to know?'

'What have they done with Tom?'

'He's in one of the rooms, with somebody with him all the time.'

Making sure he didn't slip away, presumably, although James's description of Tom's condition made that seem very unlikely. At least he was alive, though.

I thought fast, wondering what I could do to keep him that way. There was only one solution that I could see. I had to get him away from the gang.

'The rest of them are having a cook-up in the kitchen?'

'That's it.'

'How can I reach Tom's room without them seeing me?'

He told me.

'Right. I'm coming for him. Don't you get in the way, James. There's no need for you to be involved.'

Any more than he was already, I meant. I didn't want him to be collateral damage.

'Now,' I said, in answer to his next question. 'I'm coming now.'

'You're going there?' Senga said.

I nodded and stood up to put on my jacket. 'Logan's boys are having a feeding frenzy in the kitchen, apparently. So I'm going to try to get Tom out while they're at it.'

'I'll come with you.'

'Uh, uh!' I shook my head. 'You'll only get in the way. Sorry, but I don't want to have to worry about you, as well as Tom.'

She took a moment to swallow her indignation. Then she said, 'If you get him out, what then?'

'*When* I get him out, I'll bring him back here. After that, we'll have to see.'

She nodded, as if at last I was making sense.

'Then Tom can tell you himself what it's really all about,' she said.

'That would be nice.' I gave her a hard look. 'I'll look forward to that.'

But she disconcerted me by suddenly leaning forward and brushing my cheek with her lips. 'Take care!' she said, for all the world as if she meant it.

Chapter Twenty-Four

THE SNOW IN the street was up to my knees now, and it was still coming down heavily. I trudged through it as fast as I could, head ducked down, shielding my eyes against the icy wind driving the snow into my face. Nobody else was about, and the only lights came from above the entrance to The Shepherd's Rest.

I turned into the narrow alley separating the pub from the nearest house and made my way towards the back of the building, looking for the fire escape. Taking care on the slippery metal steps, I climbed to the emergency door on the second floor. As James had promised, it was ajar. I placed my fingers in the crack, eased the door open and slipped inside the building. Then I paused for a few moments, heart pounding, while I secured the door behind me and wiped the melting snow from my face and eyes.

The corridor was bathed in emergency light only. James had said that no rooms were occupied on that floor. I could hear plenty of noise coming from downstairs, though. Party time, it sounded like. The uproar suited me fine. Any sounds I made were not going to be noticed. I just hoped James was coping.

I made quickly for the stairs and dropped down to the floor below. Three of the rooms towards the end of the corridor had light spilling from open doors. One of them, according to James, contained Tom and a guard. Probably the end one, the room furthest from the staircase.

A quick glance into the first open doorway revealed an empty room. I moved on. It was the same with the second room. Tom had to be in the next one. I glanced quickly round the doorway and saw a lone figure curled up on the bed, encased in a quilt.

I stepped inside and glanced around. Confirming that there was no one else there, I made for the bed. As I reached it, Tom suddenly sat up, eyes wide open. I slapped a hand across his mouth and shook my head to warn him to be quiet.

Then I heard the sound of a cistern flushing. My pulse shot up towards the ceiling. The guard!

I swung round and stepped away from Tom, my eyes on the door that had to lead to an en suite bathroom. As it started to open outwards, I slipped behind it, hugging the wall.

One of the biggest men I had ever seen came out of the bathroom. He seemed to fill the entire space. But it was no time to marvel or wait for him to see me. I stepped forward and stamped heavily on the back of his legs.

With a cry of shock he crumpled to the floor. I hit him on the head, but not hard enough. He looked over his shoulder and began to get up. A gun appeared in his hand. That was enough for me. I kicked him in the head with all the power I could muster, and he dropped with a heavy crash, flat out.

'Come on, Tom!' I snapped. 'Get up.'

The poor lad was dazed. He stared at me, bewildered. I reached for him and pulled him upright. 'Now, Tom! We've got to go.'

I reached for his jacket on a chair beside the bed and wrapped it round him. 'Come on, son!'

He took some shifting but somehow I got him moving. I hustled him into the corridor and along to the staircase. We paused there for a moment while I checked. No one was in sight. I pushed Tom up the stairs.

We reached the second floor emergency door and got through it without a problem. I closed the door gently. Then I steered Tom down the fire escape, which was a bit tricky in the conditions. Cold, wet, slippery metal, with a coating of icy snow. But we made it without falling flat on our faces.

Grabbing Tom by the arm, I hustled him along the street, doing my best to erase our footprints as we went. We reached the cottage and I pushed Tom inside. Then I shut and locked the door with an almost overpowering sense of relief. For a moment I sagged against the wall while I caught my breath and waited for my pulse to return to something like normal.

'Here you are!' Senga called, coming down the stairs.

That was enough to make me rally and straighten up. I pushed Tom into her arms.

Warmth, coffee and familiar, friendly faces all helped bring the lad round.

'Where's this?' he asked as Senga led him through to the kitchen.

'Somewhere safe,' she said.

I had my doubts about that, but I kept them to myself.

'Was I ever glad to see you!' he confided over his shoulder to me, as if we were the best of friends.

'I'll bet.'

I felt like kicking him up the backside, but it wasn't the time for that. Besides, he'd suffered enough already. He didn't really need me to dump on him as well.

We had a cup of coffee while we warmed up, wound down and swapped stories. Then I suggested to Senga that we took turns to grab a couple of hours' rest each. She volunteered to take the first watch. Tom was excluded from the discussion. Apart from him not being up to it, I just didn't trust him. It would be a serious shock to me if he ever did the right thing.

'Wake me in a couple of hours,' I told Senga.

She nodded.

I flopped onto the bed in the room next to Julie's and must have gone to sleep more or less immediately.

I woke up reluctantly.

'It's time, Frank,' Senga whispered.

'What time?'

'Five. You said to …'

'Thanks. Now you try to get some sleep.'

'I don't think I can.'

'Just rest, then. You need it. Where's Tom?'

'With Julie. They're both asleep.'

I nodded and got up. Senga lay down.

'Anything happening out there?'

'Nothing.'

I made some coffee and took it to the window in the living room. If anything, it was even darker outside now. The lights were out at the pub. The snow had stopped. Nothing was moving. I stood drinking my coffee, thinking about the day to come.

Our isolation wasn't going to end soon; that much was clear. Even if no more snow came, it would be many hours before the ploughs could cut a way through the drifts on the moor. So nobody was going to get in or out of the village for some time. We would have to keep our heads down and try to evade Logan's people somehow.

I sighed. It threatened to be a long day, with no certainty of outcome.

Chapter Twenty-Five

BIG CYRIL STAGGERED into the doorway, propping himself up against the wall with one hand. Blue swore and jumped to his feet, scattering crockery.

'Steady!' Eddie cried as plates of bacon and egg cascaded over him. Then he turned and gasped as he saw what Blue was looking at.

'What happened?' Blue demanded.

'The kid got away,' Big Cyril said.

'How long ago?'

Big Cyril shook his head and promptly grimaced, regretting the movement. 'I don't know,' he admitted. 'Not long, though. Half an hour, max.'

'The kid did this to you?' Blue asked with incredulity.

'Not the kid. Someone else. I went for a slash. When I came out of the bathroom he was behind the door, waiting for me.'

'Who was he?'

'No idea. I didn't really see him.' Big Cyril looked longingly at the table where the rest of them were eating. 'Anything left?'

Blue studied him for a moment, thinking. Then he shrugged and said, 'Help yourself.'

The others made way for Big Cyril. Blue thought it through a bit more. So someone had helped the kid get away? Whoever it was, he had some balls, taking on Big Cyril – and besting him. He had no idea who it could have been, but they'd better find him fast – and get the kid back.

Blue found the landlord in his office. 'You said there was nobody else here?'

'That's right,' James said, looking puzzled. 'There isn't.'

'No guests, no staff – nobody?'

'Nobody else at all,' James said. 'Just me and you lot. Why? What's on your mind?'

'Somebody just jumped one of my men and beat him up, and then took the young lad we were looking after.'

James shook his head and looked sceptical. 'You're having a laugh!'

'You sure there's no one else around?' Blue asked, giving him a cold eye.

'If there is, I've never seen him – or her.'

Maybe, Blue thought. Maybe not. 'For your sake, that had better be true,' he said. 'We're going to search the place. You come with me, and bring the key to every room.'

The search didn't take long – it wasn't a big building. They found nobody. All they found was evidence of how the kid and whoever had helped him got out.

'This door normally kept shut?' Blue asked, studying the emergency door on the second floor.

'Absolutely.'

The wind was whistling through a slight gap around the edges. James took hold of the bar and pulled the door properly shut. Blue opened it again and peered out. He could see the snow had been disturbed on the fire escape. Someone had been out there not long ago.

'This is a one-way door,' he said, studying the mechanism. 'It can only be opened from the inside, right?'

'That's right,' James agreed. 'It has to be that way. It's just an emergency door, leading to the fire escape.'

Blue slammed the door shut again. 'So now we know how they got out.'

'And it's easy enough to get in,' James said with a shrug. 'The front door's been open all night.'

'Maybe,' Blue said thoughtfully.

'You know it has. Are we done here?'

'For the moment.'

Blue turned to lead the way back to the kitchen.

'I was wondering,' James said, 'how did you get the name Blue? It's a funny nickname.'

'Keep wondering,' Blue said coldly.

Back in the kitchen, he announced the plan.

'Whoever hit Big Cyril and helped the kid get away, they haven't gone far. They can't have got out of the village even. So we'll grab some sleep now, and in the morning we'll start looking for them.'

'They could be anywhere,' Manny complained.

'How many houses are there in the village?' Blue said sharply. 'Twenty? Thirty, at the most. We'll search them all. They won't be hard to find.'

He turned to James. 'Give me your mobile.'

'My phone? What for? I need it.'

'No, you don't.' Blue stared hard at him. 'Where is it? I won't ask you again.'

Reluctantly, James said, 'It's in the office.'

'Go and get it. Eddie, go with him. If he gives you any trouble, shoot him.'

The wraps were off now, Blue thought grimly. No more Mr Nice Guy. Along with that went the need to prevent news getting out of the village.

The failure of the landline system was a godsend, in that sense. It meant regular phones and computers were out of operation. That left mobiles. Bloody mobiles! It was a pity they'd ever been invented. He shook his head and sighed. They would just have to gather them all in. Then his own mobile vibrated. He took it out, frowned at the screen and answered.

'Monsieur Bleu?' a familiar voice demanded.

He walked away from the others as he began responding in French to the queries he had been anticipating for some time.

Manny raised his eyebrows when he caught Eddie's eye. Eddie just shrugged and looked away. He didn't know what was going on. He didn't even want to know.

Chapter Twenty-Six

THE SNOW REALLY did seem to have stopped. It was hard to be sure now the whole village was without lights, but it was no longer swirling past the window. I sat waiting, wondering what Logan's men would do next. It was anybody's guess. Probably they wouldn't decide themselves until morning, but they would know they had to move quickly. They couldn't afford to be here still when the emergency services broke through the snow drifts, bringing the police with them.

My phone began to growl and vibrate. I pulled it out of my pocket and glanced at the screen before I answered it.

'Yes, Bill?'

'Are you coping?'

'Just about. I've got Tom Steele away from Logan's gang. Now we're all together in a cottage in the village. We'll be OK till daylight, I think. But I don't know after that.'

'There's no way you can get out?'

'None at all. It's very cold and the snow's really deep. We're a long way from anywhere else, as well. Ten, maybe twenty miles. We wouldn't last long or get far on foot. I'd probably be able to manage myself, but not with Tom and the two women.'

'Well, you're going to have to hang on for a while yet,' Bill said. 'Colleagues in Northumberland tell me the ploughs are working on the road overnight but they don't expect to get through to the village much before midday.'

I grimaced.

'What do you think? Can you manage?'

'I hope so – somehow.'

'You'll have to. That's all there is to it. The emergency services are fully stretched all over the north of England. I don't even like to think about Scotland. Fire and rescue, ambulances, councils ... But the police will be there as soon as the ploughs break through. I've been assured of that.'

'Tell them they'll need an armed response unit. Logan has four or five men with him, and I'm pretty sure they're all armed.'

'Understood.'

Bill was quiet for a moment. Then he said, 'I'm involved in this myself now, as you know, because of the attack on the Steele house in Marton. The Chief has told me to liaise with the Northumbrian Force, and do whatever it takes.'

'Good.'

There was some comfort in the knowledge that Bill was involved. It gave me a boost.

'I've not had much time to look into things down here,' he added, 'but there's something very odd about the Steeles' situation.'

'What's that?'

'For a start, you were right. Sources tell me Steele had some sort of business dealing with Logan before the trouble broke out.'

'Before Logan's son was killed, you mean?'

'Yes. Then it went pear-shaped, all of a sudden.'

'And Logan really is a big-time criminal? You've confirmed that?'

'Yes. He's a career criminal. The law hasn't been able to catch up with him yet, but there isn't any doubt about that. He's been lucky. He's been thumbing his nose at the Met for many years, aided by expensive lawyers. I still can't understand why Steele would be involved with him.'

'Me neither. Any idea what their shared interests are?'

'None at all. But I'm working on it.'

'I've got a new name for you to look up, Bill – Blue. The guy in charge of Logan's gang in the field is called Blue.'

'Unusual name.'

'Yeah. But that's all he ever gets called, apparently. He's fortyish, black hair, strong build, and has a commanding presence. Ideal leadership figure, in fact.'

'It sounds like you've met him,' Bill said cheerfully.

'I have. He and a bunch of his thugs paid me a visit before I left Risky Point. They warned me off getting involved.'

'You should have listened to them.'

'I've thought that myself.'

There was a brooding silence. Then he rang off, leaving me to ponder another of life's little mysteries. Why hadn't I taken Blue's advice?

If I'd known then of Steele's involvement with Logan I might well have done. In fact, I would have turned Josh down in the first place. But it was too late for that now. If we all got out of this village safely, that would be the time to think again. My commitment to the Steeles wasn't open-ended.

When I turned back to the window I realized that something was changing out there. The blackness was fading to dark grey. I could see the outline of buildings across the street now. I even fancied I could make out the bulk of the hotel a little further away in the gloom. Another hour and things might start to happen.

'Anything going on?' a quiet voice behind me asked.

'No, nothing. You shouldn't do that,' I added. 'Creeping up on people can get you shot.'

'Is that what I did? Creep up on you?'

I heard a low chuckle and then a hand was placed lightly on my shoulder. Another moment and fingers massaged my neck.

'Mm! Feels good.'

She did it a minute or two longer and then stepped in front of me to peer through the window. 'It's getting light.'

I nodded.

She pulled up a chair and sat beside me. Together, we watched the street. It looked eerie out there, as the world began to flood with a ghostly pale light. The full impact of last night's blizzard was becoming apparent now. The snow lay deep on the ground and it had been piled high by the wind against the sides of buildings. The gable end of one house was plastered

119

with it, all the way up to the eaves.

'It looks so beautiful,' Senga said.

I nodded. She was right. It did.

'Even to a non-artist,' I said. 'Cold and lonely, and beautiful.'

She looked at me and smiled. 'Jac said to be careful with you, that you're not all you seem. The apparent modesty is a performance, she said. You're more substantial than you appear on first acquaintance. More sensitive, too.'

'She said all that?'

'And more.'

'Nice of her.'

'Oh, she thinks highly of you.'

'As I do of her.'

'It's just, she said, that you live too dangerously for her. She couldn't cope with it. Running a gallery requires organization and a steady life.'

I nodded. I could imagine Jac saying that. She was right, too. I couldn't deny it.

'Whereas I,' Senga said softly, 'rather like risk and uncertainty, and even danger. They bring me fully awake. Life on the edge is best, don't you think?'

I smiled and looked at her. She smiled back. Odd, how you can suddenly feel on the same wavelength as another human being, even when the circumstances are not exactly propitious. Even when you have been told things that might have warned you off.

'Was it you that came to my house that night?' I asked, knowing now what her answer would be. 'Walked round and round it? Three times?'

She nodded. 'I wanted to see if you might be the man we needed to help Tom.'

'But you didn't see me?'

'I saw enough. I saw where you live, and I could see that Jac was probably right about you.'

'Then you told your sister and her husband?'

'They needed someone like you. So did Tom. We all did.'

I wondered. I wondered about that a lot. Look where it had got them – and me.

But at least the mystery was solved at last: Senga had been the nocturnal prowler. I could rest easy about that, at least.

'Tell me about Josh and Logan,' I said.

'All work and no play?' she said sadly, her fingers sliding down my arm.

'At the moment, yes,' I said with a wry chuckle.

'What do you want to know?'

'Finish what you started to tell me earlier. You were on about Josh's main business. And the ship.'

'Oh, yes. The ship.' She yawned and collected her thoughts. 'What do you suppose it's for?'

'I said import-export. You said just export.'

'Mostly export. Josh exports a lot of heavy agricultural and industrial machinery, most of it used. It's big business.'

'Really? Second-hand combine harvesters and industrial pumps? Stuff like that?'

'Have you any idea how much "stuff like that" sells for?'

'None at all.'

'Big bucks, believe me.'

'For used tractors?'

She smiled. 'Plant and equipment like that is very valuable. I was amazed when I found out. A used Massey Ferguson tractor can fetch a hundred grand. A one-year-old combine harvester might fetch a hundred and fifty thousand.'

'Dollars?'

'No, sterling.'

I shook my head. Not junk, then. It was a revelation.

'Then there's the industrial side,' she went on. 'A big Cummins industrial generator, a year or two old, say, is worth fifty thousand. Diggers, bulldozers, loaders ... they're all worth big money. Construction equipment ...'

'I get the picture. But he needed a ship to carry it all in. That must have eaten into the revenue stream?'

'Ships are surprisingly cheap. Not new ones. But you can get a decent little coaster like Josh's, maybe twenty years old, for a hundred thousand – not much more than a decent used tractor or combine harvester. Besides,' she added, 'some of the stuff goes by road.'

That made me think of the truck with Hungarian plates I had seen in Josh's compound.

'Where does it all go?'

'All over.' She blew out her cheeks. 'A lot to Ukraine. Some to Russia. Other stuff to dirt-poor countries like Moldova and Romania.'

I struggled to place Moldova on a map. Next to Romania, I seemed to recall. Formerly part of the USSR.

'All in Eastern Europe?'

She nodded. 'Mostly. Sometimes even to breakaway little territories that you can't really call countries, like that Russian-speaking part of Moldova that declared independence the other year. I can't even remember its name.'

No more could I, if I had ever heard of it.

'Transnistria, or something like that,' she added.

'Boy, you're a whiz at geography!' I told her.

She chuckled. 'All those places have one thing in common.'

'What? Plenty of poverty? They can't afford to buy new?'

She nodded. 'That's it. Josh saw a market. You've got to hand it to him.'

Big business, then, and no doubt expanding.

'So how did it all go wrong, if it did?'

'Ah! Now we're getting to it.'

Whatever that was, we weren't there yet. Senga broke off as two things happened.

Behind us, Tom said, 'Good morning!'

And in front of us men began to pour out of The Shepherd's Rest.

Chapter Twenty-Seven

THE FIRST HOUSE they came to was occupied by an elderly couple.

'Are you from the council?' the man asked as soon as Blue came to the door. 'We've been waiting for somebody to turn up. It's ridiculous. There's no television. And the phone's not working either.'

'No,' Blue said, shaking his head and improvising quickly. 'Not the council. We're above the council. We're national security. Now, how many people are in this house?'

'Just me and the wife.'

'Two people?'

'Yes. What's this about?'

'National security. Has anyone been to the house in the last twenty-four hours?'

'No. What's going on?'

'A dangerous man has escaped. We're looking for him. Have you got a mobile phone?'

'The wife has.'

'Show me it.'

Blue confiscated the mobile, saying it would be returned when they had completed their inquiries. Then they moved on to the next house, where it went much the same.

In the third house they encountered resistance. The occupant, a young man in t-shirt and jeans, said, 'Show me some ID.'

Blue laughed in his face. 'What do you think this is – a television programme? Answer the question. How many people are in here?'

'Show me some ID first,' the young man said doggedly.

Blue nodded at Manny. 'Show him.'

Manny took out his pistol, hit the young man across the face with it and shouldered his way into the house. The man screamed and collapsed on the floor.

'Who's here?' Blue demanded, stooping over him.

'Just me,' the man gasped.

He put his hands to his face, and then stared with horror at the blood on his hands when he took them away.

"Has anybody called at the house overnight?'

'No, nobody.'

Blue stared at him. They would soon find out if that was true. If it wasn't, he would be back.

'What do you want?' the man cried.

Blue ignored him. 'Search the place,' he told Manny and Eddie.

It was true. Nobody else. They moved on, taking another mobile with them, after issuing another warning.

'Stay here till we say you can leave,' Blue said. 'Don't make us come back and shoot you. Got that?'

The young man nodded, too shaky to speak any more.

*

Generally, however, people were cooperative and eager to help by answering a few simple questions. Blue's impromptu explanations for their presence and their inquiries grew ever more inventive.

'We've got the village on twenty-four-hour lockdown,' he said a couple of times, 'while we search for this dangerous killer. We believe someone in this village has helped him to escape and evade the lawful authorities.'

'That's terrible!' the middle-aged couple in one house said in unison. 'You'd better catch them soon.'

At another house, the husband announced that he would just grab his coat and then he would come and help.

'No thanks!' Blue said hurriedly. 'We don't want innocent civilians out here. It's not safe. Better to leave it to the experts.'

'Are you sure?' the man said with disappointment.

Blue said he was.

'Do they really believe all that stuff?' Manny asked wonderingly.

'They do,' Eddie said firmly. He didn't want Manny having doubts. 'What he's doing is providing leadership. That's what people want. Give them it, and they look up to you, and believe what you say. Like with Putin in Russia.'

'Amazing,' Manny said, shaking his head. 'Fucking amazing!'

'Only half a dozen houses to go,' Eddie said less confidently a little later. 'What if we don't find him?'

'We will,' Blue said.

Privately, Blue was thinking he would soon have to turn his thoughts to getting them out of there. The snow had stopped and the ploughs would be well on their way by now. With them, in all probability, would come the police.

He should phone Logan to let him know how things were.

Even if they found the kid again, he wasn't sure they would be able to get out with him. They certainly weren't going to carry him. Better to let him eat a bullet, and be done with it. Fuck Logan!

Then there was that phone call he'd received a little while ago to consider. They were not happy, back there, and he couldn't afford that. Time was pressing. He couldn't put them off much longer either, whatever Logan thought and wanted. They had different priorities, different agendas. He'd had to work with that fact from the start.

But he would phone Logan first, he decided. No point waiting till the snow ploughs arrived. Logan was close enough to be able to do something to help. He'd better.

'You two go on to the next house,' he told Manny and Eddie. 'You know the drill by now. I'm just going to make a phone call.'

'Who to?' Manny asked. 'The BBC Weather Centre?'

'For your information,' Blue said wearily, 'I'm going to make arrangements to get us out of here.'

'Now you're talking!' Manny said with enthusiasm. 'I hate this fucking place.'

'Careful what you wish for,' Blue told him. 'There's worse places than this.'

Eddie shivered. He knew that was true.

Chapter Twenty-Eight

'THAT'S BLUE,' TOM said, pointing to the man with black curly hair. 'He's in charge.'

I nodded. I'd seen him before. He was the one who had

starred in the theatrical performance on my doorstep the other day. I suppose I was lucky he hadn't just shot me, instead of delivering a warning. It would have saved him a lot of trouble.

'Logan isn't with them?'

Tom shook his head.

'Could he have been around without you seeing him?'

'No way!'

Logan kept well back from the action, it seemed. He hadn't been at the house in Marton either.

'We'd better keep away from the window now it's getting light,' I said, getting up and moving my chair back.

'Any chance of some breakfast?' Tom asked.

'No idea. Go and see what you can find.'

The lad wasn't my favourite person, and I certainly wasn't his carer. I still hadn't forgotten that it was his stupidity that had got us into this mess in the first place.

'Come on, Tom,' said Senga, taking pity on him. 'Let's have a look.'

I stayed where I was and watched the Blue character give his orders. Then he and a couple of his men trudged through the snow to the house next to the pub and rang the doorbell. Discussions occurred on the front step. Nothing happened. They moved on, looking for Tom, I assumed.

The ritual was repeated at the next house, and the one after that. Then there was a change in the pattern. They knocked a guy aside and barged into his house. He must have given them the wrong answer.

'Breakfast!' Senga called a few minutes later.

It seemed a good idea to grab some of whatever there was to eat before the peace of the morning was disturbed. Hopefully, I"d think of something to do when Blue came calling, as I feared he inevitably would in due course. Not answering the door wouldn't keep him at bay.

We had toast and coffee. Senga had also discovered a rusty tin of corned beef in a cupboard but none of us fancied that.

'Julie still asleep?' I asked.

Tom nodded. 'She's very tired.'

I glanced at Senga, but she said nothing. Tom probably didn't know about the sleeping tablet she had given Julie. Not that it mattered.

'You were going to tell me more about the export business,' I reminded Senga. 'Where did it go wrong?'

She winced and looked at Tom. 'Do you want to tell him,' she asked, 'or shall I?'

'Does either of us really need to?'

'I think so,' she said firmly. 'Frank has put himself on the line for us – for you especially, Tom. It's only fair.'

'He's getting paid for it.'

'Not nearly enough, if I know your father.'

'You can tell him, if you like.' He shrugged and looked away. Then he got up, saying, 'I'm going to see Julie.'

So there was just me and Senga once again. I looked at her. She shrugged and started.

'Josh got involved with Logan. It began when they met on holiday in Florida.'

'Accidentally?'

'Apparently. Anyway, they got on well together.'

I just shook my head.

'What?' Senga said, bristling. 'You don't believe me?'

'They met accidentally on holiday?' I said wearily. 'And they became buddies?' I shook my head again. 'How likely is that? But go on.'

Senga frowned, as if she hadn't considered the possibility of it not being an accidental meeting.

'Anyway, Josh discovered that Logan had interests in the same trade as he did – the export of second-hand plant and equipment.'

'Tell me you're joking! In Florida he discovered that? While on holiday?'

She smiled ruefully now. 'It does sound a little improbable, doesn't it? But that's what Anne told me had happened.'

It sounded to me like one of them must have been looking for the other. I really don't believe in coincidences.

'Tell me more.'

'Logan was experiencing difficulties with transport arrangements. So he was very interested to learn that Josh had his own ship, and that he had regular shipping and marketing agents in Europe.'

'I'll bet he was!'

'So he suggested a working relationship. Logan would send some of his stuff to Middlesbrough. Josh would ship it, consign it and take a share of the profit.'

'Nice.'

'It was, at the time. At least, it seemed to be. Usually the ss *Anne* was sailing without being fully laden, and Josh knew he could sell more stuff in Europe than he could actually source in the UK. So it seemed a perfect fit.'

'The Steele and Logan Mutual Benefit Society, eh? Then what?'

'After a while Josh grew suspicious about some of the items Logan was bringing forward. He did some checking, and found that what he had come to suspect was true. Logan was shipping stuff that had been stolen. So he confronted him over it.'

'Let me guess. Logan offered him a bigger share of the profit to keep him sweet?'

Senga nodded. 'He did. He also told Josh that between them

they had already moved on a lot of stolen stuff. He, Logan, had documentary proof of it. So Josh was complicit, and would be in trouble himself if he went to the police.

'Josh decided to go along with it for a bit longer, while he tried to work out a way of ditching Logan without going to prison himself. Frankly, he needed the money, too. Business wasn't great just then. Loans were being called in, trade was down, and profits from other sides of his business had slumped with the recession.

'Then Logan got greedy. He announced that he wanted a share of Josh's other businesses. Josh exploded and went mad. Logan laughed in his face. So did Logan's son, who was a nasty piece of work in his own right.'

I was beginning to see now how it had all developed, and could even make some guesses about what had happened next. But I waited for Senga to tell me.

'Logan's son, Bryce, decided to do a bit of pressing himself. He told Tom what was going on, and then announced that he wanted the new car Josh had given Tom for his birthday. Tom said no way!'

'He'd not known any of this was happening?'

'Not up to that point. Nor had my sister. It was all down to Josh himself.'

I could almost finish the story for myself now.

'So Logan's son and Tom squabbled over the car,' I suggested, 'and somehow Logan's kid got run over?'

Senga sighed. 'That's pretty well it,' she agreed. 'Tom couldn't say much in his own defence without exposing the whole sordid business and incriminating his father – and possibly Anne, as well. So he took the fall.'

'No wonder he's mad at Josh.'

'As is my sister,' Senga said. 'Which is where I came into it.

Anne asked for my advice and help.'

'She'd got my name from Jac?'

'Yes.'

'So you came to suss me out?'

She nodded.

'There's only one mystery remaining now,' I said.

'What's that?'

'Your name: Senga. Where's that from?'

I thought she was going to decline to answer, but after an awkward moment she said, 'I was actually christened Agnes, after some favourite aunt, but I didn't like that. Who would, in this day and age?'

She stared at me challengingly and added, 'There! Satisfied?'

'Absolutely,' I said, trying hard not to smile.

Chapter Twenty-Nine

WHEN I GOT back to the window I could see that we had very little time left. Blue and his men had completed visiting the houses on the far side of the street. Now they were crossing over to start on our side. We were the third house along, and had maybe fifteen minutes before they got to us.

I called the others together, including the newly awakened Julie.

'We could hold out for a little while here,' I said, 'but not for long. They've got enough men, and enough weapons, to force their way inside pretty quickly.'

'The police will be here soon,' Tom said. 'Just as soon as the snow ploughs get through—'

'That's not going to happen in the next fifteen minutes,' I broke in to say.

'You're being pretty damned pessimistic, Frank! What the hell are you trying to do – scare Julie?'

'Oh, shut up, Tom!' Senga intervened before I could tell Tom what I thought of him and his analysis.

'Don't you—!'

'Tom, you're being a baby,' she said sharply. 'And you're the one who got us all into this mess in the first place, remember?'

'It could be hours before anybody from outside the village reaches us,' I pointed out. 'Face it. We're on our own.'

Julie began to weep. That felt like the last thing I needed.

'So what I'm going to do,' I told them quickly, before a discussion could develop, 'is get outside and lead them away from here. If I run, they'll think I'm Tom and follow. There's woodland at the edge of the village. I can lose them there.'

'Great plan,' Senga said stonily. 'Oh, yes. You look such a lot like Tom. I can see that working.'

'I'll go myself,' Tom said. 'Then they'll know it's me.'

'We'll both go,' I said quickly.

'*You* might manage,' Senga said, looking at me and shaking her head, 'but how is Tom going to keep up with you? He won't be able to.'

In a sense that was the elephant in the room. Tom wouldn't get five yards. He wasn't strong enough.

'They've got guns, as well,' Tom said listlessly. 'I've seen them.'

Julie sobbed. Senga looked at me. I shrugged. Not for the first time, I wondered how the hell I'd got myself saddled with idiot people like Tom and his pathetic girlfriend.

'Right,' I said, getting to my feet. 'We'll have to think of something else – and fast.'

I was in the kitchen when I heard an almighty crash, followed by a man shouting and a scream from Julie. I rushed towards the door, and then stopped as Senga held up a hand.

'Right, kid. Outside – now!'

Shit! One of them had arrived, even though the main party was still two houses away.

'You should have kept away from the window,' the unseen man said with a chuckle.

I grimaced, more in frustration than anger. Bloody Tom – again!

'Get stuffed!' I heard Tom say defiantly. 'Go on – shoot me!'

I winced at that. Don't! I was thinking. For crissake don't encourage him!

Senga shook her head when I looked at her. She was out of the sight of whoever had caught Tom but she could see what was happening. I grimaced. Not good.

I headed for the back door of the cottage, opened it and slipped outside. I was under no illusions. Whatever Tom said, and whatever he did to hold things up, he too would be outside in the next minute or so.

I ran round to the other side of the cottage and waited just outside the front door. There was a commotion in the hall. Then Tom came sprawling out, landing flat on his face in the snow. Julie squealed. Senga shouted with anger, and by the sound of it got clouted again in response.

'Keep out of it!' I heard the same man snap.

Moments later, Blue came through the door, gun in hand.

There was no time to think. But his surprise was greater than mine. I grabbed the hand holding the weapon and kicked hard at his knee. His leg collapsed and he went down with a grunt. To keep him down, I hit him hard across the head with the gun.

Tom got up and kicked him a couple of times for good measure before I pushed him aside. 'Bastard!' he snarled.

By then, a couple of Blue's men were running towards us. I grabbed Tom and pushed him back inside the cottage. Then I stuck the gun in Blue's face and held up a hand to stop his men. They hesitated for a moment and then kept on coming, cautiously, as if they didn't believe I was serious. I moved the gun aside and fired a single shot at their feet.

That stopped them.

'Get back!' I told them.

Blue raised a hand towards his men and swivelled round to look up at me. 'Who the hell are you?' he demanded, shaking his head to clear it. 'You look familiar.'

'It's that Doy bloke,' one of his men growled. 'The one Steele went to see, and then we visited.'

'Ah!'

Blue was satisfied. Mystery solved. He had placed me.

'We've come for Steele's lad,' he said then, as if he was talking about emptying the rubbish bins – and for all the world as if he held the upper hand.

'That's not going to happen,' I told him.

'We'll see.' He cleared his throat, spat and then sat back and glanced skywards. I looked up too. We'd both heard it, a droning noise coming from somewhere up there.

The faint drone became louder, and then became a roar. It was accompanied by a *whop-whop-whop* sound that we all recognized. A helicopter appeared, swooping over the hills that surrounded the village. The relief I felt was indescribable. The cavalry – at last!

'You boys left it too late,' I said, grinning at Blue.

He grinned back. 'You think so?'

Then another of his men stepped out into the middle of the street and started waving the helicopter down, putting an end to my assumption that it was coming for us.

My phone vibrated. Keeping the gun in Blue's face, I fished it out. The noise was such I had to press the loudspeaker button to hear.

'The plough's nearly here!' James shouted excitedly. 'They're just outside the village.'

Blue heard too. He looked at me with a calculated look and said, 'How about a deal?'

By then three of his men had guns pointing at me. I wondered how close the plough really was, and if the police were with it. I couldn't be sure.

'You shoot me,' Blue said calmly, 'and they shoot you.'

Probably.

'Or maybe they just shoot you first, and worry about me afterwards?'

Even more likely.

'Neither of us gets out alive,' he added unnecessarily.

He was right. I should have got him inside the house before his men arrived. Then I might have been able to hold on for a while. Out here I couldn't. Stalemate. Or worse.

I stepped back and motioned to him to get up. He got to his feet and walked away, ushering his men in front of him. Neither of us said another word.

The chopper came down fast and settled in the middle of the street, making a great booming noise that reverberated around the village and shook the walls of the cottage. Its rotor blades created a snowstorm that filled the air with swirling white clouds. The houses on the other side of the street vanished from view.

I stepped back into the doorway of the cottage and watched. Within two or three minutes the gang were all gone. The chopper powered away over the rooftops and then over the hills, with its infuriating *whop-whop-whop*. As the storm it had created settled, I turned to watch a snow plough arrive outside The Shepherd's Rest. A council lorry followed, then a second snow plough and more vehicles. But there was no police car.

I went inside to see how Tom and the others were. They all seemed fine, shaken but relieved to know help was here at last.

'So that was Blue,' I said with a grimace.

Tom nodded. 'Prat!' he said.

I wasn't sure if he was aiming that barb at Blue or at me, but I ignored it anyway.

'How are you?' I asked, turning to Senga instead.

'My other eye will be black, as well, now,' she said, squinting and giving me a rueful smile.

I smiled back and gave her a hug. She seemed to welcome it.

My abiding thought as things settled down was to wonder why no one had sent a chopper for us. We could have been spared all this. Most of it, anyway.

Chapter Thirty

BY THE TIME I got back outside, things had changed even more. It looked as though the Red Army had arrived, fresh from a battle in the winter of 1944–45. A third snow plough had appeared, and a fourth, along with another wagon and an assortment of mechanical diggers, tractors and utility vehicles. Local people were pouring out of their houses to greet the rescuers, who looked suitably celebratory and heroic as they acknowledged the delight their breakthrough had inspired. Soon, I fancied, James would throw open the doors of The Shepherd's Rest to add to the sense of occasion.

'No police, though?'

I turned to find Tom at my shoulder.

'Not yet,' I said with a forgiving smile. 'No doubt they'll be along soon.'

'So I was wrong about that, as well,' Tom said bitterly. 'And you were right.'

'We can't have been top of their agenda, Tom. That's all. They have a lot on at the moment. But don't let it worry you.'

'It's one more thing, though, isn't it? I just fuck up all the time.'

'Come on, Tom! That's no way to think. You've had a bad time this past year, that's all. Things are looking up for you now.'

He didn't seem convinced but there were limits to my ability to cheer him up. Fortunately, I noticed something else I'd been right about: the throng was moving towards James's front door.

'Come on!' I said. 'Let's get the others, and see what's happening in the pub.'

Coffee. Mostly it was coffee happening, sometimes with a shot of something else to liven it up. Breakfast orders were also being taken. James's staff must have arrived for work.

Already a celebration was in progress, the rescue party just as excited as the locals.

'Sixteen hours we've been going,' one of the drivers announced triumphantly to me. 'All through the blizzard. But we made it!'

'You deserve more than coffee,' responded Julie, who seemed

to have woken up at last.

'Aye, well,' the man responded modestly. 'James knows that. He'll look after us.'

Senga grinned happily at me. 'Party time!' she said.

I nodded. But my thoughts had gone back to the helicopter. I was wondering where it had taken Blue and his gang, and I was still wondering why one hadn't come for us.

Twenty minutes later flashing lights outside announced the arrival of the police.

'At last!' Tom muttered.

'Better late than never,' Senga said.

I didn't bother saying anything. I had never really held high hopes of the police rescuing us. I had known all along that we were on our own.

I shouldn't have been astonished when Bill Peart walked through the door, but I was. At least he wasn't first man in. He followed a uniformed officer in an inspector's cap and a couple of other uniforms, obviously all local men. I could see more of them in the doorway.

The inspector stood in the middle of the room, and by his very presence commanded attention. The room fell quiet. He announced himself with a couple of wry asides about having been delayed by the conditions and then got on to serious matters.

'We know you've had a difficult night in this village, and we're determined to get to the bottom of it. First, though, is there anyone injured or ill? We have paramedics with us, and they will deal immediately with anyone requiring medical attention.

'After that, we will start taking statements from each of you. If people wish to return home in the meantime, that's fine.

We'll catch up with you there.'

It didn't seem that there were any serious casualties, but there were plenty of cases of bruised feelings and egos – and plenty of people eager to talk about them. Tom wasn't the only one feeling badly used.

I looked around. Nobody was heading for the door. Everyone who had made it here seemed intent on staying put, determined to have their say. They'd probably all had enough of being incarcerated in their own homes.

Introductions over, Bill Peart made a beeline for our little group. Having established who everyone was, he took me outside for a chat. I noticed armed police in and around a couple of Range Rovers. We could have done with them a little earlier.

'Logan's gang got away, I gather?' Bill said.

I nodded. 'A helicopter came for them.'

'A helicopter?'

'That's right. You never thought of sending one for us?'

'We didn't have one available.'

'Logan found one.'

'His budget must be bigger than ours. What time did they leave?'

'Just before the snow ploughs arrived. Actually, that was what saved us. They were searching the houses, one by one, and had just found us. We got lucky.'

'You said they were armed?'

I nodded. 'All of them, probably. That's why I advised you to bring an armed response unit. Here's a pistol I took off Blue, by the way.'

I handed it over.

'Northumbria weren't terribly interested,' he confided. 'There's people in trouble all over the region, and they took some convincing as to how serious the situation here was.'

He was being unusually frank. Internal police matters were usually a no-go area. But his explanation suggested why help had been a bit late arriving.

'What are you doing here anyway, Bill?'

'Assisting with inquiries,' he intoned, 'given my role in the ongoing investigations in Cleveland.'

'That can't have been easy to arrange.'

He looked thoughtful for a moment. Then he said, 'Our chief plays an occasional round of golf with theirs.'

'That right? And are they both Masons?'

He glared at me and changed the subject.

'Have you worked out what this is all about?' he asked.

'Not really. What I told you was right enough, but there's more to it than that, a lot more. Business dealings between Steele and Logan went wrong, it seems. A budding relationship turned sour. A boy got killed. Scores are being settled.'

'Is Logan really trying to kill the Steele boy in revenge?'

'That's a tough one. It's what I was told, and was brought on board to prevent happening. Now I don't know. They could have killed him easily enough last night, when they had him for several hours. So why didn't they?'

Bill didn't know the answer to that any more than I did.

'They wouldn't even have had to shoot him,' I added. 'They could have just left him out in the snow for hypothermia to do the job for them. The lad was knackered.'

'Maybe Logan wants the satisfaction of doing it himself?'

I grimaced. That was entirely possible.

'Or he wants to use the lad as a bargaining counter?' I suggested.

'To get what?'

'I don't know. I'm still working on it.'

'That's all very well,' Bill said tartly. 'But just remember

140

which side you're on.'

It was a good point. Which side was I on, though? I was no longer quite sure.

Chapter Thirty-One

'Is he your cop friend?' Senga asked. 'The one you told me about?'

'Yes. DI Bill Peart.'

'Don't tell him what I told you about Josh's business problems, will you?'

I just looked at her for a moment. Then I sighed. 'Maybe it should come into the open? Maybe that would help?'

She shook her head vigorously. 'No! It wouldn't. I'm quite certain of that. Not now, anyway. Tom would never forgive me.'

I wasn't sure that Tom's sensitivities were a big concern for me, but they seemed to be for Senga. So I agreed to keep quiet, at least for now.

Presumably she thought the problems could be sorted, or perhaps she just didn't want to see her entire extended family behind bars. I didn't either, actually. Tom might have been a pain in the backside the past few days, and Josh an idiot, but criminal prosecution, financial ruin and imprisonment weren't going to help anybody. That's how I looked at it. There's the law, and then there's justice. But then, I'm not a cop.

So we gave Bill what information we felt we safely could, and then he reluctantly agreed to persuade his local colleagues to let me take our little group back to Cleveland. We were glad to be on our way, but we hadn't reached the end of it. There was still Blue and Logan to deal with. And now there was also a frustrated DI Bill Peart, who knew we weren't telling him everything we knew. From a personal perspective, I didn't know which bothered me the more.

We left as we had arrived, in two cars. Senga was taking Julie home to wherever it was she lived. Tom was with me. I wasn't sure what I was going to do with him. Taking him back to Josh and Anne in Marton, and confessing failure to look after him properly, wasn't an appealing option. But what was the alternative? I didn't fancy just holing up with him somewhere else. That probably wouldn't work any better than it had the first time.

It took us twenty minutes to clear the cars of snow and dig a way through to the track cleared by the ploughs. Then we were off. Tom and I led the way in the Volvo, with Senga's Golf not far behind.

From the start, it was obvious why the rescue convoy had taken so long to reach the village. I had never seen such snow in England. The ploughs had dug only a single-track lane across the moor and on either side the drifted snow was at times ten-feet high. It was like driving through one of those Olympic toboggan runs. What we would have done had we met a vehicle coming the other way was anybody's guess.

Tom was understandably subdued. He had a lot to think about. I let him be and concentrated on the driving, which at times was tricky. The gritter following the plough had done its best but there were sections of road where the grit must have run out. Then we were on ice. It was a time to be cautious. I wanted to get us away safely, not be stranded somewhere until someone came along to pull us out of a snowdrift.

'I hate fucking snow,' Tom said suddenly.

The sound of his voice was so unexpected I almost jumped.

'You don't think it makes the world look a better place?'

'Definitely bloody not!'

Each according to his taste, I guess.

'What are we going to do?' he asked then. 'Now we're out of there, I mean?'

'What do you want to do? Go back to Marton?'

He shook his head. 'That's the last place I want to go at the moment.'

I took my foot off the throttle, slowed and changed into second before heading down a long slope that looked particularly icy. I saw in the mirror that Senga held back and sensibly kept her distance all the way to the bottom.

'I need some thinking time,' Tom continued, as if he hadn't even noticed the driving conditions. 'There's a lot to sort out.'

'Like what? What's changed?'

He sighed. 'Nothing, I suppose. It's just that I've still got it all to sort out.'

He was right about that. I doubted if Logan had changed his mind, and Blue and his gang were out there somewhere. So Tom was still in danger. It was good to hear him thinking of it as his problem, though. That made a welcome change.

'Can we just go back to your place?' he asked.

I was surprised, but tried not to show it. 'Yes, if that's what you want.'

'Thanks. It is.'

In a way, it wasn't a bad idea. We both needed to rest and recover while we worked out what to do next. One thing I knew for sure: it wasn't over. This story had plenty of legs left in it yet.

Tell me about the accident, Tom – or whatever it was.'

'What do you want to know?'

I shrugged. 'Just tell me what happened. That will do.'

'It was ridiculous,' he said, shaking his head. 'It was just a stupid situation that shouldn't have ended the way it did.

'Bryce Logan had been hassling me for a while, and hassling Julie as well. He wanted her and he wanted the car Dad had given me. It wasn't going to happen, any of it, but he wouldn't give up. He told me he was going to make trouble for my family if I didn't give him the car. He was going to bring us all down.'

'By doing what? Telling the police about the shipments of stolen plant and equipment?'

'He never spelled it out, but that was definitely one possibility.'

'But it would have dropped his own father in it, surely?'

'That wouldn't have worried him. He hated his father, and vice-versa. They couldn't stand each other.

'Anyway, one night I'd been out with some mates for a drink. He was waiting for me when I got back to the car. He said he was going to take it – just like that! I laughed at him. Then a couple of my mates came up and he walked away.

'He must have followed me to Julie's. Later, when I came out of her place and got in the car, he was there again, waiting for me. He wanted the keys. I told him to get lost.

'When I started the car, he walked into the middle of the road and held his hand up to stop me. He had a gun in his other hand. I kept going. I assumed he would get out of the way. But he didn't. I hit him. I wasn't going fast but he hit his head on the road, and that was that.'

'You said all this in court, presumably?'

'Some of it.'

'Which bits did you leave out? The bit about Bryce having a criminal father who was in business with your father? Or the bit about Bryce wanting your car and your girlfriend, and making threats?'

'What else could I do?' Tom sighed and shuffled in his seat. 'I didn't want Mum and Dad to lose everything they had worked for all these years. I didn't want them to be sent to jail. I just pretended Bryce was a stranger who stepped off the pavement in front of me.'

'And you'd been drinking. You were over the limit, I believe. Well over?'

He nodded.

'What did your dad tell you to do?'

'He wanted me to tell the full story – about Bryce hassling me, and making threats.'

'But stopping short of the bit about him and Logan being in business together?'

Tom nodded. 'He didn't think it was necessary to mention that part.'

'I bet he didn't!'

He sighed and added, 'But I knew that wouldn't work. If I gave the cops a bit of the story, they would work out the rest of it eventually. They would just keep on pulling at the thread till they had the whole damned lot.'

I thought he was probably right about that.

In the space of just a few minutes, my opinion of Tom had begun to change. No wonder Senga was so supportive. He was an astute kid who had done his best for everyone but himself.

I could see now why he was so mad at his father. It was Josh's doing that had got him into all this in the first place. I could also see why Anne was so fed up with her husband. Poor Josh. Everybody had it in for him, and you couldn't say it was undeserved.

'Dad was on about getting me an expensive lawyer but I

wouldn't have it. I knew that once that happened it would be difficult to keep all the other stuff quiet. I told him I would refuse to be represented by someone like that. I was just going to plead guilty. Mind you, I might have changed my mind if I'd known I would get a year in custody. I assumed I would just lose my licence and get fined. That didn't seem so bad.'

That irritated me.

'What? You thought running somebody over, and killing them, was just like a speeding offence, or being a bit over the limit?'

He winced but said nothing. There was nothing he could say. I changed the subject.

'You mentioned that Bryce and his father didn't get on?'

'No, they didn't.'

'Father and son?'

'It's not that unusual. Anyway, Bryce wasn't Logan's real son. He came with his mother when she got involved with Logan. I don't know who his real father was. I don't know if he even knew himself.'

'Fathers and sons, eh?'

'Me and Dad are different.'

'Of course you are. I've seen you both in action.'

Tom smiled ruefully.

'We'll go back to Risky Point,' I said, 'but I want to see your dad. We've got to sort out a way of getting Logan off your back.'

'How are we going to do that?'

'We'll think of something,' I said with more confidence than I felt.

Chapter Thirty-Two

'I KNOW WHAT he'll be doing,' Tom confided.

'Who?'

'Dad. He'll be doing what he said he would. To get me off the hook, he'll be offering Logan a bigger percentage from the next shipment. It's a big one, apparently, due out on the first of December.'

In three days' time, then. That was interesting.

'What's in it?'

'The usual, I suppose. I heard Dad say it was particularly valuable, though. So there's something special about it, but I don't know what.'

'Would giving Logan a bigger share work?'

'No idea. But Dad thought there was a chance. He wanted me out of the way for a while, in case things went wrong. I guess that's where you came in.'

All this put me in a bit of an ethical quandary. My client's interests come first usually, but not always. I wouldn't be party to shipping stolen property abroad. I had to draw the line somewhere.

On the other hand, I couldn't let the Steele family go down the tubes either. I didn't know Josh, but there was Anne to consider. More than that, there was Tom's life to protect. I had made a commitment to do that, and once committed it was a matter of principle with me to stay the course. Conscience and professional reputation wouldn't have it any other way.

I decided to speak candidly to Josh as a sensible first step. Then I'd have to see. Hopefully, we could sort something out that suited us both. Hopefully, too, I would find a way of squaring things with Bill Peart – and avoid getting myself locked up.

*

Just north of Morpeth, the snow thinned out and some of the lanes of the A1 had been cleared. The going was better but I decided to pull into the town for a rest and a cup of coffee. The Golf followed us obediently as we looked for somewhere to park. A half-empty supermarket car park fitted the bill nicely.

'Thank goodness!' Senga said, as we met them getting out of the Golf. 'I was in danger of going down with snow blindness.'

'And caffeine withdrawal symptoms,' Julie added.

They both seemed in good spirits. I was pleased about that. Julie actually seemed better – and more normal – than at any time since I had first laid eyes on her.

We had coffee in a busy Costa on the main street. Then Julie said she needed to do some shopping. Tom said he would go with her. So Senga and I had another coffee and talked.

'How did you find the drive?' I asked.

'Fine. It was a bit difficult at first, coming over the moor.' She shivered and added, 'I've never seen such snow!'

I had to agree. 'The North Country, eh?'

'You're not kidding. So what's next, Frank?'

'Tom and I have been talking about that. I need to see Josh, I think. I want to find out what he's been doing to get Tom off the hook – if anything.'

'Are you and Tom OK now?'

'Better, I think. He wants to come back to Risky Point with me. I said fine. Perhaps he's decided we're both on the same side, after all. He's told me about the accident, by the way, and a bit more of the background.'

'Good.'

Senga thought for a moment and then said, 'I think you're right about talking to Josh. We do need to know what he's been doing.'

'We?'

'I'm in this as much as you, Frank.'

I took a moment. Then I smiled and said, 'Good! I hoped you'd say that.'

My phone started buzzing at that point.

'Yes, Bill?'

'Where are you?'

'Morpeth. Drinking coffee with the gang.'

'Nice. I'm still here in the snowy wastes.'

'Making progress?' I asked cautiously.

'Not really. I'm just catching my breath while the local officers sweep up the remaining interviews.'

I waited. He hadn't rung to tell me that.

'Remember asking me about that Blue character?'

'Yes?'

'I've come up with something. At least, someone has. The name meant something to somebody.'

'What have you found?'

'Well, it may not be the same man, but there is a guy known to French police as "Monsieur Bleu".'

'With a criminal record?'

'Not as such, but he's known to be part of the southern mafia. He's half-British, apparently. He works out of Marseilles, as an enforcer, but he's been off the local scene for a little while. And – get this! – the rumour is that he's gone to the UK on business. Interesting eh?'

'Very. I wonder if that could be our man?'

'I think it might.'

Senga looked at me expectantly after the call.

'Does Josh have any French connections?' I asked. 'That you know about?'

'Possibly. I don't really know. Why?'

'It might mean nothing, but Bill Peart tells me that a Monsieur Bleu is known to French police as part of the Marseilles mafia.'

'And that's Blue, is it?'

I shrugged. 'I dunno. But it might be.'

Chapter Thirty-Three

THE HOUSE IN Marton had been fully restored, a remarkable feat in such a short time. Gerald was worth his weight in gold when it came to getting things done.

Josh and Anne said nothing about it. They were far too pre-occupied with getting their son back in one piece, and eager to hear all about his experiences. After a decent interval for the family reunion, I managed to draw Josh aside for the serious discussion he and I needed to have.

'First,' I said, 'I have to admit that I didn't do a very good job of looking after Tom. I should have handcuffed and leg-ironed him so he couldn't run out on me.'

Josh smiled ruefully. 'He can be an awkward so-and-so, when he wants.'

'I gather you found that out for yourself after the so-called accident?'

That raised eyebrows. 'What do you mean, Frank?'

'Tom has told me what really happened.'

'About the accident?'

'And other things. The shipments of stolen machinery along with the legitimate trade, for example, and your business dealings with Logan.'

'He shouldn't have,' Josh said, looking peeved. 'Some things are better kept in-family.'

'Not these things, Josh. Not if you want my help.'

He looked unsure about that for a moment. Then he said, 'Well, it's water under the bridge now. Thanks for what you've done for us, Frank. We'll sort it out ourselves from here on.'

I shook my head. 'It's not over, Josh.'

'It is for you,' he said tartly. 'You've done what we asked you to do, and you've been well paid for your trouble. My cheque is in the post.'

I shook my head again. 'I don't think so. You don't get rid of me that easily.'

'So what now? You're going to blackmail me? Join the queue!'

'I signed on to protect Tom. The job is not finished.'

'It is for you,' he repeated.

Again I shook my head.

'What have you done to get Tom out of this mess, Josh? Anything at all?'

'Logan will withdraw his threat against Tom's life, if that's what you mean. We'll reach an understanding with him.'

'You and Anne?'

He nodded.

'So what will you do – offer him a better deal on your illegal exports? Perhaps you've done it already?'

He looked absolutely furious now. He was livid with mounting rage.

'You go too far, Doy! This has nothing at all to do with you. What I do in my business is my business. Clear?'

'If you think I'm going to stand idly by while you and Logan conspire to export another load of stolen property, you're living in cloud cuckoo land. It ain't going to happen, pal.'

He slowed down and studied me. 'So what are you going to do – blow the whistle? You took our money, remember?'

'Josh, I'll be quite happy to tell Cleveland police what I know, and let them be the judge of whether or not I did anything illegal.'

'You can't do that.'

'Watch me.'

We stared at one another for a few long moments. Then he said with a sigh, 'What do you want? More money?'

I shook my head. 'Not money, no. I want to know what steps you've taken to safeguard Tom. Then, if necessary, I want to work with you to figure out a way of undoing them, and finding a legal way of protecting Tom – and you and Anne, as well, for that matter.

'I accept that you didn't know what you were getting into initially, and ideally I would like to see you come out of it a free man still, and with a business that's still afloat.'

I had reached him. I could see that. His anger was subsiding. He had his thinking head on now, and could see he wasn't going to be able to brush me off as lightly as he'd hoped. He probably regretted ever having involved me, but what could he do now? My threat to unload to the police was a potential disaster for him, his business and his family.

'Come and sit down, Frank,' he suggested. 'Let's talk.'

He led me through to a room that served as an office. There, he opened a drinks cabinet disguised as a filing cabinet and motioned to me to select something. I shook my head. We sat down around his desk and stared at one another.

'Just tell me what's going on,' I suggested. 'It can't be worse than I already think.'

'Oh, it can!' he assured me with a wan smile. 'Far worse.

I can almost guarantee it. What do you think of Tom, by the way?'

'Tom?' I chuckled and shook my head. 'At first, I thought he was an ungrateful, spiteful, egotistical, spoilt little rich kid. Now? Now I can see where he's coming from, and I rather like him. He's done well by you and Anne, even though he has a lot to complain about.'

Josh nodded. 'You can say that again. I got him into all this, and he wouldn't let me get him out of it. I'm proud of him.'

He looked challengingly at me.

'I understand all that, Josh. Just tell me what you've been doing to try to keep him safe. Time isn't on our side, if the first of December is as important as Tom says it is.'

That earned me another malignant look. Clearly, he questioned my right to know that date, and resented the fact that I did know.

'The shipment,' I said impatiently.

'I know what you mean.'

He sighed again and shook his head. Then he started.

'I'm going to offer Logan the proceeds from the entire shipment, in exchange for dropping the vendetta.'

'You haven't done it yet?'

He shook his head.

'Will it work, do you think?'

'The shipment is worth a lot of money, but who knows?'

'Tom seems to think Logan isn't really all that bothered about avenging the death of his son – his stepson, rather.'

'That seems to be true.'

'You and Anne misled me.'

He shrugged, implying that they had done and said what they had thought necessary at the time. Perhaps it had been.

'So money might do it,' I continued. 'How much is the

shipment worth?'

'In round figures?'

'Round figures will do.'

'Twenty million?' He shrugged again. 'Maybe a bit more.'

'Sterling?'

He nodded.

I was impressed. It was a lot of money for what still seemed to me like a shipload of old junk.

'That's without being able to price Logan's own contribution,' Josh added.

'The stolen stuff?'

'Yeah. That's worth maybe another five to ten million. Plus whatever it is that he's adding this time that I don't know about.'

'Oh? What might that be?'

'I dunno.' Josh shook his head. 'But I'm told there's a special item this time that he'll bring forward only at the last minute.'

'And you've no idea what it is?'

'None at all. But that happens from time to time.'

'Where's it going?'

'France – Marseilles.'

That really got the gears in my head working hard. Marseilles, eh? Where the mysterious Blue might be from.

Then something else came to mind. Almost with horror, I recalled what Jac had said about Senga being involved with a French guy a little older than her. Coincidentally, that would make him the same sort of age as Blue. Coincidentally? Two separate Frenchmen on the scene, both involved with the Steele family?

Or was there only the one? Surely not. Was that possible? It couldn't be!

But it could, I thought with grim realism, even if she had sustained a black eye.

After all, how much did I really know about Senga, the wild child of Jac Picknett's acquaintance? Next to nothing, basically.

How come she was even here? Being Tom Steele's aunt didn't seem to explain it. Even Josh had been astonished to learn she had joined us in that remote Northumbrian village.

No, poppycock! Ridiculous. What was wrong with me? It was just coincidence. It had to be.

'Right,' I snapped. 'I'm coming with you, Josh, when you make Logan your offer.'

'You're not!'

'I am. Get the bloody meeting arranged.'

Chapter Thirty-Four

LOGAN WANTED TO meet at a convenience hotel north of the river, just outside Billingham. Josh looked at me. I nodded agreement. Josh said yes, and put the phone down. We would meet Logan the next day at noon, the venue and the time both his choice.

'Do you know the place?' Josh asked me.

I nodded. 'It's nothing special. Just part of one of those nationwide chains.'

'Is it safe?'

'Safer than your house,' I said with a grin.

He chuckled and switched on his phone again. 'I'll call my head of security. Get him to take a few of the boys there for protection.'

'No,' I said sharply, shaking my head. 'You do that, and Logan won't show up. We want him there.'

Josh paused, index finger poised over the keyboard. 'Why won't he?'

'He doesn't need a pitched battle in a public place. He knows he's got us on the run. Thinks he has, anyway. He can dictate terms.'

'What if he brings a team of his own?'

'We can handle it.'

'How?'

'By making him believe he's going to get what he wants. We're not going to make trouble – not at the meeting, at least.'

Josh didn't like it. But he switched the phone off, the call unmade. Then he walked across the room to stare out of the window, watching the light fade.

'Logan doesn't want you,' I pointed out. 'He wants either Tom or your business. Maybe both.'

'Aye, you're right,' Josh said with a weary sigh.

We sorted out a few details. Then I set off for Risky Point. Tom decided to stay in Marton with his folks, after all. That suited me. I sensed we were moving into the end game now. I preferred being free of encumbrances, which is what Tom was. If I was to sort all this out, Tom had to be parked somewhere safe, where he would be looked after. Leaving him in Marton gave both Josh's security team and Anne something to do.

Somehow the situation seemed much simpler now. Admittedly, Tom was at risk still, and so was Josh's business. Logan remained at large, as did Blue and his boys, and presumably revenge and aggrandisement were still on the agenda. That was the downside.

On the upside, the fact that Logan was interested in

negotiating at all indicated that the situation wasn't black and white. He wasn't in nihilistic mode. There were things he wanted that he still hadn't got. That made the situation, from Josh's point of view, potentially open to reason and negotiation – and, hopefully, solution.

My own position was a little different to Josh's. I wasn't entirely on his side. I did want to secure Tom's safety, but I wasn't going to allow Josh to continue to support a criminal enterprise. In particular, I was determined that the ss *Anne* was not going to sail on the first of December and deliver stolen plant and equipment to foreign criminals. Somehow I was going to stop that. Somehow.

That still left a lot of uncertainty, of course. Like how to do it.

I needed to satisfy Bill Peart, as well, and keep him happy without sending Josh and Anne down in flames.

I had no idea if it was all going to be possible. We would just have to see. One step at a time. First, I would attempt to get Logan off Tom's back, and off Josh's as well.

There was also Senga and her Frenchman to think about. What to make of that? Nothing or something?

All in all, my plate was full.

Blue took the call with some trepidation. He explained the situation as best he could. The response wasn't long in coming.

Enough! he was told. If you need to, get rid of him. It's up to you. Use your discretion.

So that was that, he thought with satisfaction. The way ahead was clear now.

Chapter Thirty-Five

SENGA WAS WAITING for me at Risky Point, which was a surprise.

'Where's Tom?' was the first thing she asked as she got out of her car to join me.

'He decided to stay in Marton, after all. I think he wanted to reassure Anne that he was all right. Probably he wanted to see more of Julie, as well.'

She nodded.

'So what are you doing here?' I asked. 'You couldn't trust me to get Tom back safely?'

She grinned. 'Not only that.'

'Oh? Well, now you're here, how about coming inside?'

'I thought you'd never ask.'

First, we had a look over the cliff edge at the raging sea. It wasn't high tide, but that wasn't far off. The vast waves boomed like cannon fire as they hit the base of the cliff and the spray almost reached us some three hundred feet higher. A lesser spirit might have shuddered.

'How wonderful!' Senga said, grabbing my arm.

I nodded, pleased. But, then, I'd always known she would like it here. Hadn't she told me herself that she liked living on the edge?

'We live dangerously here,' I said, turning away to lead her back to the cottage, 'just as you prefer.'

She laughed.

'Who lives in the other cottage?'

'Jimmy Mack, an old friend. He's an almost retired fisherman.'

'Isn't it difficult to be a fisherman and live on a cliff top?'

'Yep. That's why he's almost retired. Mind you, on a good

day I still help him get out in his boat.'

'Where is it?'

'At the foot of the cliffs. There's a path down there. Well, not exactly a path, but you can get down there. It's a bit of a scramble, mind.'

'Can we go...?'

'Not today,' I said quickly. 'I'm cold and I'm tired.'

She laughed and tucked her arm into mine. I saw Jimmy Mack watching from his doorstep. He lifted a hand in greeting and Senga gave him a wave back.

'Don't encourage him,' I said.

She laughed happily.

I didn't feel quite as light-hearted as she obviously did. I still had the meeting with Logan to look forward to. There were also my newfound doubts about Senga to process. All the same, the immediate pressure was off, and I didn't mind admitting it was good to have her there with me. I just hoped my suspicions turned out to be as ridiculous as I had begun to think they were in her presence. I'd been wrong about people before. Plenty of times.

Between us, we put together a supper. It didn't look like much to start with. Just some pasta, salami, cheese, a baguette out of the freezer, a bowl of olives, a salad Senga made from a few vegetables in the dark corners of the fridge ... Suddenly the table was overloaded. I added a bottle of Chianti.

'My!' Senga said admiringly. 'You do rather well for yourself here.'

'Well ...' I paused to look at the assembled spread. I was impressed. 'One does try.'

We got started. Conversation did, too. I asked her about her work, her art.

'I'm a painter,' she said simply.

'Professional?'

She nodded. 'Well, I make a living out of it. Sort of. Not a very good living. That will have to wait until I'm dead, and the value of my paintings goes through the roof. But I manage. I do a bit of casual driving for Josh, as well. That helps financially.'

'Ah! So it was you driving the Audi when they brought the Volvo?'

She laughed. 'Yes, that was me. I wanted another look at you!'

'You should have got out of the car. I could have given you an autographed photo. How do you know Jac Picknett, by the way?'

'Oh, we go back a long way, Jac and I. We met at art school, and since then we've bumped into each other from time to time. I've even exhibited in her gallery. She lived much like me to start with, but eventually she decided she would rather run a gallery than try to eke out a living from her own paintings. She's done well, too.'

I nodded. Senga's story was what I had expected to hear. It was a good story, too. People who follow their star deserve respect. It's a rare person that can do that for more than five minutes.

'You live locally?'

'Great Broughton, a village near Stokesley. I rent a little place there.'

'So you paint landscapes?'

'No, not at all.' She shook her head. 'My work is abstract.'

'Oh?' I said, letting disappointment into my voice. 'So you didn't come here to paint the cliffs?'

She smiled and said, 'I came to see you.'

'And Tom, of course?'

'And Tom. But he's not here, is he? So I'll have to make do with you.'

And suddenly we both knew where this was going. Not yet, though. There were still some practicalities to sort out and detain us first.

As for my doubts and suspicions about her, well, they hadn't entirely disappeared. They were still there. It was just that they were not quite so pressing. They didn't seem to matter so much now I was home in Risky Point.

'I'm going with Josh to meet Logan tomorrow,' I told her.

'Oh?' Her eyebrows rose with surprise. 'What to do?'

'I'm hoping we can negotiate a deal that will lift the threat to Tom.'

'By?'

'Josh wants to give Logan the proceeds from this forthcoming sailing.'

'What – all of it?'

'Yes. We're talking big money, apparently, but if it gets Tom off the hook ...'

Senga frowned thoughtfully. 'The total shipment will be worth many millions of pounds.'

'So I understand.' I shrugged. 'Josh seems to be able to afford it.'

She was non-committal.

'There's something else to consider, as well,' I added, watching her closely for any signs of a reaction.

'What's that?'

'I understand there's a French connection this time. There's a special consignment that Logan won't tell Josh about. It's going to Marseilles, apparently.'

There wasn't a flicker. She just shrugged and said, 'How do you know that?'

'Josh told me. He knows it's coming, but he doesn't know what it is. What I'm wondering is if that special item is coming with its own protector.'

'Is that likely?'

'It's certainly possible, given where it's going. If there really is a mafia connection, I would say it's even likely. I also believe their representative could well be Blue – or Monsieur Bleu, as they might know him.'

To an extent, of course, I was fishing. And I saw nothing in her face to indicate any knowledge of what I was suggesting. If anything, she seemed uninterested in all the speculation, even weary of it, which I found encouraging.

She looked at me now and grimaced. 'Oh dear! Please be careful tomorrow, Frank, won't you?'

We looked at each other for another moment or two. Then she eased herself up from her chair and came into my arms. All our problems were left then for another day.

Chapter Thirty-Six

DESPITE MY WARNING, Josh had arranged to have a security team in the vicinity. I spotted them as soon as we rolled into the car park. Oh well, I thought with a grimace. No doubt Logan would have people here, as well.

'They stay out of it,' I said.

'What? Who?'

'Don't come over all innocent with me, Josh. It doesn't suit you. Before we get out of the car, I want you to phone Marty and tell him they are only to appear if you call them. I don't want to risk this meeting getting off to a bad start. OK?'

He shrugged but didn't argue. Instead, he took out his phone and delivered the instruction.

'One other thing, Josh. Treat this as a proper negotiation. Bargain with Logan. Don't just give him everything he wants at the outset. If you do, he'll walk right over you. Be business-like about it. OK?'

He grinned. 'Right, boss!'

'I mean it, Josh. Don't show your hand at the outset.'

'It's my son we're going to be talking about,' he pointed out testily.

'And I want him to stay alive almost as much as you do.'

Having got that point over, we sat in silence for a moment. If I could have got away with it, I would have come alone. My worry was that Josh would be so emotional he would blow it.

Still, it was too late for wishful thinking or regrets. Josh was here. I'd just have to make sure we played our hand well. It wasn't a great hand, but it ought to be possible to win a few tricks with it. That was all I really wanted, and hoped for, from this encounter.

That, and to play myself in with Logan.

Josh knew I wanted to secure Tom's future, but he didn't know what else I wanted. And I wasn't going to tell him. 'Ready?' I asked.

Josh shrugged. 'Yeah.'

'Let's go, then.'

It was the kind of hotel where you had to wonder how they stayed in business. Midday in midweek, and scarcely a guest in sight. The reception staff would have been bored out of their minds if they hadn't been able to play games on their computers.

Josh had booked a meeting room. We were shown to it. Logan had not arrived yet. That gave me the opportunity to check it for bugs and other hazards. Josh watched with astonishment.

'You can't be too careful,' I told him. 'And this is one of the things I do for a living.'

He shook his head and said nothing.

We waited. Josh ordered coffee. We waited. The coffee came. I sat down with mine. Josh paced up and down with his. We waited.

'How much longer?' Josh asked, running a hand through what was left of his hair.

'Relax, Josh. Sit down. We're staying for as long as it takes. We don't want to give him any excuse for backing out. Order a newspaper if you're bored.'

Instead he phoned his security chief, who said nobody had arrived in the car park yet.

'He's not coming!' Josh fumed at me.

I shook my head. 'You're wrong. He's already here.'

'What? Marty said—'

'He's here, Josh. He's just letting you worry yourself to death. It's a good tactic.'

He snorted, and began to walk up and down even faster. I was content to play the waiting game. They were not going to unsettle me.

'By the way, Josh, what do you know about this French connection Logan has?'

He just looked at me.

'You told me about it. Remember?'

'I don't know anything about it. Just that Logan is intending to send something to Marseilles. Why?'

I shrugged. 'It's interesting. I'm wondering what it can be.'

He shook his head and continued pacing up and down.

Nothing to do with him, he seemed to feel. That lack of curiosity was probably what had got him into trouble in the first place.

'Something else, Josh. Does Senga have a stake in the business?'

'What business? My business, you mean?'

I nodded. He stared at me as if I wasn't right in the head.

'She drives cars for you, I believe?'

He snorted and said, 'That's all she does. How could she possibly have any involvement?'

'I don't know. Just asking.'

He stared at me suspiciously. 'What's on your mind?'

'Nothing. Well, Senga, I suppose. She's single, is she?'

'As far as I know.'

'No boyfriend?'

'Look, Frank, she's Anne's sister for God's sake! That's all I know about her.'

'What about the French boyfriend? Know him?'

I got the impression this was driving him crazy. He glowered at me and shook his head again.

'Ask Anne, if you want to know anything more about her – not that she's likely to be able to tell you much. Senga goes her own way. I don't know if the thing with the French bloke is still on or not. Ask Anne.'

I yawned. 'Just asking. Filling in the time. We could play snap instead if you like?'

Josh didn't think much of that either. But at least I had confirmed that there was or had been a French guy in Senga's life. Jac had been right about that. It was something to think about.

Half an hour after the scheduled meeting time, the door suddenly opened and in came the man I assumed was Logan, accompanied by the man I knew to be Blue.

Josh spun round.

Logan paused in the doorway, eyes fixed on me, and demanded, 'Who's he?'

'My associate, Mr Doy,' Josh snapped back. 'Who's he?' he added, with a nod at Blue.

'Blue, his staff sergeant,' I said when it didn't look like Logan was going to answer. 'Or is it Monsieur Bleu?'

Blue gave me a cold, hard look.

I smiled back at him. 'We've already met a couple of times, haven't we?'

He didn't reply.

'Anyone else coming?' Logan asked.

'Not that I'm aware of,' I said. 'Let's get started. Coffee's on the table over there.'

Logan and Blue sat down across the table from me. Neither bothered with the coffee. Perhaps they suspected we'd doctored it.

Josh sat next to me.

'Do you want to check the room?' I asked Logan.

He shook his head. 'Done it.'

That confirmed my theory that he had arrived early, if not last night. He was an astute man. I hoped he was also capable of seeing reason.

'Let's get started,' Josh said, parroting my suggestion.

'OK by me,' Logan said amiably enough. 'What have you got in mind?'

Blue, I had met. Strong and tough, he was comfortable in jeans and a checked shirt with the sleeves rolled up. Cold and snow didn't bother him. Nor did working in unfamiliar territory. I guessed he would be equally comfortable wherever he found himself.

Logan was different, and different to what I had expected too. Dressed in a smart business suit, and without the Essex tones I had anticipated, he gave the impression more of a white-collar crime boss than an East End gangster. Without making it too obvious, I tried to take my measure of him while the preliminaries were being conducted.

Josh weighed in at full throttle. 'I want this vendetta to end. The damage to my properties and the threats to my son – I want it all to end now. What do you want from me to make that happen?'

Logan laughed in his face. 'What makes you think you can bring this to an end just like that? It's the murder of my son, Bryce, I'm concerned with.'

'Oh, it is, is it?' Josh said testily. 'And what about my son, who you've been trying to kill?'

'What's your price?' I asked, butting in before Josh lost his temper altogether and Logan walked out.

Logan looked at me as if I was something unpleasant he'd noticed on the sole of his shoe. 'Who the hell are you?' he demanded.

'Doy. He's the PI I told you about,' Blue intervened.

'Oh, this is him, is it?' He stared hard at me and added, 'Keep out of it, Doy. This is nothing to do with you.'

'You must have a price in mind,' I insisted quietly, ignoring the attitude. 'All this can't be pure nihilism.'

'Oh? Fancy words? A learned man!'

'We're here to negotiate,' I said calmly. 'If you don't want to talk to us, why did you bother coming? I assume there's something you want. What is it? Let's see if we can make a deal.'

Logan shook his head and chuckled, but not with amusement. 'Just listen to him,' he said conversationally to Blue. 'Lecturing me. Who does he think he is?'

Blue's face was expressionless as he, too, continued to stare at me.

'No threats,' I said, 'but if we can't reach a deal, we're going to be coming for you. Make no mistake about that.'

I felt Josh stiffen beside me but I didn't look. I just hoped his nerve held.

'Oh yes?' Logan said with a mocking smile. 'You and who else – the Steele private army?'

'Working together with Cleveland police, we'll bring you down, if that's what we have to do. The Steele family have had enough. They're prepared to take the consequences of involving the police, if needs be. They are not prepared to live like this any longer.'

Logan looked angrily at Josh now. 'Do you hear what he's saying?'

'I hear him,' Josh said quietly, keeping it tight.

Good man! I thought.

'As I understand it,' I said cheerfully, 'you've got a few million pounds' worth of merchandise on the ship. You'll lose that if we can't negotiate an end to this situation we find ourselves in. Make no mistake. We'll hand the ship over to the authorities.'

'And lose your own stuff, as well?' Logan said.

'We're prepared to do that.'

'I'd like to hear it from Josh himself,' Logan said, seemingly unimpressed, but quieter now. He was thinking.

'So you don't believe we'd do it?' I took out my phone. 'Do you want to see me speed-dial the cops?'

'Go right ahead!'

Blue leaned forward and spoke for the first time. 'That won't be necessary,' he said quietly.

He eyeballed Logan, who visibly calmed down. That made me think. So Blue had a say here? I wondered what gave him that. Perhaps he wasn't working for Logan, after all.

'We accept that you have certain objectives in mind,' I continued, addressing Logan. 'The most important of them obviously concerns your late son.'

'Your son—' Josh began, as if he was about to say what he thought of the late Bryce.

I overrode him.

'We understand all too well how you feel about the sad loss of your son in that tragic accident, but killing Josh's son in revenge is not going to bring Bryce back again. That said, we would like to explore the common ground between us, to see if there's some way Josh can make amends by offering some form of compensation.'

'Wow!' Logan said. He looked at Blue and at Josh, and then he laughed. 'Is this guy for real?'

'He speaks for me,' Josh said wearily.

'You should have said you were bringing a lawyer, Josh. I'd have brought one myself.'

'So what do you want?' I asked bluntly.

'What's on offer?' Blue fired back.

Without looking at Josh, I said, 'You get to keep your own cargo on this next shipment plus twenty-five per cent of the Steele consignment.'

Logan chuckled and glanced at Blue.

'We estimate the Steele share is worth £20 million,' I continued. 'So that's another five mil for you, on top of whatever your own cargo is worth.'

Blue shook his head. 'Five million? You must be joking. That's nowhere near enough.'

'What are you looking for?'

Suddenly we were debating figures, which was a lot better than trading insults and absolutes, and talking about killing

Tom. I was the one doing the negotiating for our side. Josh was still there, but I didn't look round to check or to draw him in. I wanted him to stay silent.

'The whole thing,' Logan said eventually. 'Everything.'

I didn't know if he had the shipment in mind or Josh's entire business empire, but I didn't ask in case we got an answer we didn't like.

'The whole twenty mil?' I said with incredulity.

'No!' Josh said suddenly. 'No fucking way!'

'Take it or leave it,' Logan said amicably, seeing Josh rattled now and believing he held a winning hand.

Blue and I stared at one another. I knew from the meeting at Risky Point that he was a consummate performer. I knew from the meeting on the doorstep in the snow, his life possibly in danger, that he was a cool negotiator. I also knew it was no good just caving in. That would only embolden them to demand even more.

On the other hand, I didn't want them walking out on us either.

'Forty per cent,' I said quietly.

Blue shook his head.

I glanced at Josh. He stared at me without much interest. He looked as if he had given up.

'Fifty per cent, then,' I said. 'And that's a damned good offer!'

'Not for blood money, it isn't,' Logan said in a fierce whisper. 'You're paying for the murder of my son, remember.'

So that's what he thought it was? Blood money. Well, perhaps he was right. In any case, however much it was, it was better than having to hold a funeral for Tom.

'Josh has to get something out of it,' I urged. 'See reason!'

Logan and Blue both just stared at me. They knew they had us now. They could sense they had won.

'OK. The whole damned lot,' I said with a sigh.

I turned to Josh and said wearily, 'You OK with that?'

He just shrugged.

'Josh?'

Reluctantly, he nodded.

'Right. It looks like we're done here,' I said, standing up. Josh remained seated.

'Not quite,' Blue said.

'Oh?'

'There's an extra load to be taken on board the ship.'

'What is it?' Josh asked then, looking up.

'Nothing to do with you,' Blue said.

'The ship is pretty near full.'

'If necessary, we'll take something off to make way for it. One other thing. Instruct your skipper that the first port of call will be Marseilles, as I believe Mr Logan has already indicated.'

Josh shrugged. It didn't make any difference to him now. He had lost ownership of his own cargo.

'OK,' I said. 'Marseilles it is.'

Blue nodded at me. Then the pair of them got up and left. We stayed where we were.

We gave them a few minutes to get clear. Then I said, 'Come on! Let's get the hell out of here.'

Josh was pretty subdued. On the way back to the car, he said, 'How did I do?'

'Great. But keep looking miserable, in case anyone's watching.'

'Some negotiator!' he said out of the corner of his mouth. 'You realize what you've done? My whole bloody shipment down the tubes!'

'Just remember this,' I told him patiently. 'We've won.'

Chapter Thirty-Seven

'So we've won, have we?'

'Just get in the car, Josh.'

We buckled up and set off.

'Tell me how we've won, Frank. Seriously, tell me.'

'We've got Tom off the hook.'

'There is that, I suppose.'

'Come on, Josh!'

He sighed and nodded. 'That's the important thing,' he admitted reluctantly.

We drove on silently, each of us with his own thoughts. Josh was coming to terms with losing twenty million quid's worth of gear. I could understand that that was difficult for him, even though in the end Tom's life was all that really mattered.

For my part, I needed to keep Josh on board while I sorted out how to keep Tom alive and yet stop the shipment reaching Marseilles, without putting the Steele family in prison. All we had done so far was win a little time. First, though, Josh's ego needed massaging.

'You played your part beautifully, Josh. You should be on the stage.'

'You think so? I prefer cinema, actually.'

'Movies, then. You should be in the movies.'

'I'll have to think about it,' he said with a grin.

I began to relax. He was coming round.

'Fancy something to eat?'

'Why not?' Josh yawned. 'Might as well eat before I go bankrupt.'

'Is it as bad as that?'

He squinted as he did some mental arithmetic.

'Just for the record, Frank, Logan's stuff on the ship is all stolen, and won't have cost him a thing. Mine is legal and honest – and paid for. So I'll be down a lot of money.

'At least Tom will be OK now, though, won't he?' he added, seeking reassurance.

'He should be. Logan's been offered more than he could ever have dreamt of getting.'

'Yeah,' Josh said, nodding. 'Tom will be OK now. So I suppose we did win.'

'Now you're talking!'

He reflected a bit more and then said, 'But the loss I'm taking on the shipment will clean me out. I'll have to start all over again.'

'Can you do that?'

'I suppose so,' he said with a shrug. 'I've done it once. I can do it again. I'll have to put most of my businesses into receivership, though. There's no way I can accommodate a loss like that and keep them all afloat. Still, we've got Tom out of it. That's the main thing.'

Actually, I didn't really know about that. I wasn't so optimistic. We did have an agreement, but would it stand? I wasn't so sure. What happened the next time Logan wanted to make an illegal shipment? It could be the same thing all over again.

But I was determined Logan was not going to benefit from even this shipment. I wasn't going to allow him – or Blue, for that matter – to get away with it. I'd never be able to go fishing with Bill Peart again. I had to find a way of stopping them.

'What are you thinking?' Josh asked over lunch at the pub where we'd stopped. 'I can see you're turning something over in your mind.'

'Do you really want to know?'

'I do. I'm sure it concerns me, and mine.'

'What I'm thinking is there's no way I'm going to allow Logan and Blue to get away with it. You know that, Josh, don't you? Tom's the priority, but I'm not prepared to let criminals export a shipload of stolen goods.

'Besides, if they bring it off once, they'll be back for more. We've got to find a way of stopping them for good.'

'And renege on the agreement?'

I nodded. 'Just as they will, if and when it suits them. They're career criminals, remember – not legitimate business-men or upright citizens.'

'Peace-in-our-time all over again?' Josh said wearily.

'Well, it's not a legitimate business contract, enforceable by law, Josh. You've got to get that into your head.'

'So how have we won?' he said, pushing away his half-eaten meal.

Just as we got back into the car, Josh received a phone call. It went on the speaker. So I heard every word.

'We've got your boy,' Logan said. 'Make sure you honour your side of the bargain, and then we might keep ours.'

That was it. The call ended. Josh swung round to stare at me, wild-eyed and distraught.

'It makes no real difference,' I said with a grimace. 'It's what I expected.'

'We'll deliver the shipment,' Josh said grimly. 'You can forget about not going through with it. We'll do exactly what we agreed.'

That was not how I saw it, but I nodded anyway. Then we set off for home.

Chapter Thirty-Eight

I TOLD JOSH to turn around and drop me off a little way down the road from the hotel.

'What for?'

'I'm going back there. I want to know where they're based. So I'm going to track them when they leave.'

'They'll have gone by now.'

I shook my head. 'I don't think so. Marty would have told you if they had.'

'How are you going to track them on foot?'

'Have a car dropped off at the hotel car park for me – the sooner the better. Tell them to leave it unlocked, with the keys under the floor mat.'

'It'll take time. They'll have left ...'

I nodded. 'Just do it, Josh. Phone Gerald now.'

He pulled into a lay-by and made the call. I got out.

'Where will you be?' he called.

'Don't worry about that. I'll find the car.'

There was a cycle track beside the road. I set off to jog the last half-mile or so back to the hotel. It was hard going in the slush and the snow. Long before I got there I was feeling ill-used, and thinking the next job I took would be somewhere warm.

Thankfully, the light was poor by the time I arrived. Heavy cloud suggested there was even more snow to come, and soon. It was a poor day to be hiding in bushes and waiting, which was what I was going to have to do.

I settled down beside an electricity substation, with dense shrubbery in front of me. From there, I could see the whole of the car park and also the main entrance to the hotel. There was another entrance, for service personnel and deliveries, on the far side of the building, but the access road came round to the front anyway. That meant I could see whoever left the building, whichever door they used, unless they took off across country.

I was soon cold. It – the day – was cold. Winter was setting in. I turned my collar up, tucked my hands inside my coat and settled down to the stakeout. Hopefully, Logan would not keep me waiting too long. If he intended making a night of it, I would have to think again.

Twenty minutes later two cars nosed into the car park, one after the other, and then separated. One, a Ford Mondeo, parked. The driver got out and walked across to the other car, a BMW. He slid inside and it took off.

I nodded with satisfaction. I had a car.

Just after five, by which time it was completely dark and I was shaking with the cold, Logan and Blue came out. They were on their own. As soon as they hit the pavement outside the main entrance to the hotel, a Mercedes pulled up for them. Perfect timing.

The Merc got under way, and I ran for the Mondeo. The keys were where I'd wanted them to be. The engine started first turn. I was heading out of the car park little more than a minute after Logan.

I had seen them turn right. I did too, and sped up to close the gap and find them in the column of traffic that was building up now we were in the rush hour. I couldn't see the Merc. I was worried that their lead was too big. I jammed my foot down and swung into the fast lane.

A couple of miles down the road, I caught up just as the Merc was slowing down to take a slip road. I crossed back into the inside lane and followed them up to a junction. They turned right. I let them go while a couple of cars crossed. Then I pulled out and headed in the direction they had taken.

They didn't go far. Ten minutes later we trundled through quite a large village – Greatham. Out the other side, they turned onto a single-lane track that led to a farmhouse set back a couple of hundred yards from the road.

Feeling greatly relieved, I made a mental note of the approaches to the turn-off and kept going without slowing down. I was satisfied. Finding their base was a big positive to take out of the afternoon.

On the drive home to Risky Point I had plenty of time to reflect on the day's events. Gradually I came to a new and brutal conclusion. For all this to stop, it seemed to me now that Logan had to be made to disappear for good. Blue, too. There was no other way of guaranteeing peace of mind for the Steele family. Temporary setbacks were not going to do it. Arrest and imprisonment wouldn't either. One way or another, a permanent solution had to be found.

I didn't want to upset Bill Peart, which meant I couldn't just shoot them. I had to come up with something cleverer than that. What, though?

Then there was Tom, both short term and long. Josh was right about one thing: Tom was the priority. I couldn't risk anything that might make his situation worse.

I didn't spend much time wondering how Tom had managed to get himself abducted again. The lad had a talent for being in the wrong place at the wrong time, and doing the wrong thing. I knew that full well, and to my cost.

As it happened, Senga told me the details when she arrived at Risky Point soon after me.

'They kidnapped him from Julie's, and told her to say nothing to anyone if she valued his life.'

'He was at Julie's place?' I asked incredulously.

'What?' Senga said defiantly. 'He's not allowed out, or something?'

I sighed. 'It would have been better if someone in the family – if not Tom himself – had thought about security. Where the hell was Marty?'

'Tom just left and went there, without telling anyone.'

'That trick again, eh?' I shook my head. 'Well, we can't do anything until he's safe.'

'Agreed,' Senga said, undaunted. 'So what's the problem?'

I gave her an impatient look but managed to keep my cool. She probably knew already what I thought of her hapless nephew, fine young man though she obviously thought him to be.

'The problem is how to keep Tom alive and at the same time avoid letting Logan walk off with a shipload of plant and machinery, none of which belongs to him.'

'Float off, you mean.'

Luckily for her, she was smiling when she said it.

'Float off,' I agreed. 'Look, why don't you make yourself really useful and open that bottle of wine you brought?'

'Yessir!'

Later, after a makeshift supper, we returned to the main agenda.

'So what happens next?' Senga asked.

'Next, I meet Blue tomorrow morning. We will await the arrival of his special consignment, for which we must find a place on the ss *Anne*. Then, if all is correct, Tom will be released – maybe.'

'And then?'

'The following night the ship sails, unless I can find a way of stopping it.'

'You're really intent on doing that, aren't you?'

'I am. I don't want to see Tom dead, Josh ruined and in jail, and Anne in tears, but there's no way I can allow that ship to reach its destination. My little business, such as it is, is honest and legal. It always has been. I'm going to keep it that way.'

'All right, all right! Enough said. So what are you going to do? Let's be practical here.'

'I'm working on it.' I smiled ruefully. 'The only idea I've had so far is to make Logan and Blue disappear. Unfortunately, I can't just shoot them, and I haven't thought of another way of doing it.'

Senga frowned. 'It might be easier just to make the ship disappear.'

'I don't think that's going to happen either.'

'No, perhaps not. What's this mysterious cargo Blue wants to bring on board?'

'No idea. All I know is that it must be something big if he needs a ship to carry it in. It must be valuable, as well.'

She nodded. 'Blue seems to be a significant figure, doesn't he?'

'Significant?'

'Well, he seems to carry some clout.'

That was true. I'd seen it during our negotiation. Even Logan had deferred to him at certain points. He was a hard, tough man, and he wielded influence.

'Do you want me to come with you tomorrow?' Senga asked.

'Thank you, but no,' I said firmly.

'So I don't have to get up early?'

I shook my head.

'Let's go to bed, then.'

I had discovered by then that it was a mistake to think you knew what Senga would say next. She was just full of good ideas. At the time, though, I was still underestimating her, a situation that soon she was to put right – and not in bed either.

For the moment, at least, my reservations and suspicions about her seemed to have been forgotten.

Chapter Thirty-Nine

IT WAS ONE of those hard mornings. Eventually it would be light and perhaps the sun would shine, but not for hours yet. The nights are long at the tail-end of the year. Senga got up with me soon after six, when it was still dark and frosty. After a quick breakfast, she helped me scrape the ice off the windows of the car while the engine was warming up. Then I gave her a kiss and got in. With the heater blasting away, I set off, crunching over the frozen snow.

I was supposed to meet Blue at ten, and was in good time. I arrived at Josh's compound early, made my presence known to the ever-present Gerald and then went over to the jetty to see what was happening on the ship. That was where Josh was, helping his skipper with the logistics. My job was to accompany and accommodate Blue when he turned up. That way, maybe we would get Tom back. Maybe.

There was a lot of fog hanging over the river that morning, and patches of ice covered the puddles on the pitted concrete surface of the jetty. I shivered and tried not to think of how soon the glistening sides and deck of the ship would turn to ice once it left the Tees and headed out into the cold wastes of the North Sea.

That might well be soon, I realized. It looked to me as if there wasn't much work left to do aboard the ss *Anne*. In layman's terms, the ship was full, crammed to overloaded. Only a small space had been left on the main deck. We would have to see if that was big enough for whatever Blue was bringing to the party.

I still didn't have an answer to my problem of how to stop the ship leaving its berth. Maybe some obscure customs requirement might do it? Or some other bureaucratic hurdle. But when did that ever stop the mafia? A tip-off to the police might do it, but that would bring everyone down. I still wasn't at the stage where I was ready to countenance the nuclear option.

Blue turned up exactly on time. I was waiting on the jetty when a Toyota Land Cruiser turned in the gates of the compound and accelerated across the tarmac towards me. It stopped and Blue got out. He walked briskly towards me.

'There will be a delay,' he announced.

'Why's that?'

'The transport hit slow traffic. It will be another hour.'

I nodded. 'Fine. Where's the boy?'

Blue jerked his head towards the Land Cruiser.

'He's in there?'

'As our guest,' he added with a ferocious grin. 'Under armed guard.'

'That's not necessary, surely?'

'Just keep your end of the bargain.'

I wondered if there was any way I could get Josh's men to surround the vehicle and release Tom. I decided against even trying. The compound was likely to be full of corpses if we did that – most of them ours.

'So what do you want to do?' I asked.

'Wait,' Blue said.

'Where?'

'Here is fine.'

I could see he meant it literally. Tough guy, eh? OK. We would wait here together. I was damned if I was going to offer him a seat or a coffee, never mind shelter. We would just wait, here and together.

'What's the load like?' I asked.

'That's not your concern.'

'It is if you want it on the ship. We need to know how big it is, for a start.'

He thought about that but didn't offer any information. I changed my mind about waiting with him.

'Right,' I said. 'I'll see you at eleven.'

I turned to walk over to the offices.

'Stay here!' he snapped.

'What for?'

'Stay here, where I can see you.'

I gave him a big smile. 'Nice!'

But I was more intrigued than concerned. His edgy response suggested he was under pressure, as well. It was good to know. Maybe I could work on that.

'You'll have to tell me if there's space for your load,' I said. 'Be reasonable, for crissake! How big is it?'

He weighed up his answer. I had hit a nerve. He knew I was right, but he was damned if he would admit it. He didn't want to give anything away until he had no choice. My intent was to give him no choice.

'You will see at eleven,' he said.

I shrugged. 'Fair enough. But, in that case, expect delays.'

'There will be no delays.'

'There will. How easy do you think it is to configure the load on a ship? How long do you think it takes to move stuff around and arrange things so the ship won't capsize once it hits a big wave?'

He thought about it some more and then volunteered, 'It's big enough.'

'How big?'

He screwed his face up in concentration, blew out a cloud of condensation and finally added, 'It's on a low-loader.'

'And does the whole lot need to go on board?'

He nodded.

'Jesus! I'd better check what space is available.'

'Stay here. If there isn't enough room for it, something will have to come off. We'll sort that out when the load arrives.'

More delays, then. Big delays. It didn't bother me. He was the one who might find delay created difficulties. I had all the time in the world.

On a low-loader, eh? Interesting. That meant a big crate of some description, or a container, perhaps. Full of what? I was no closer to knowing that. But one thing I did know was that there was no space at present for a low-loader on board the ss *Anne*. So there certainly would be a delay. Maybe that would give me a chance to think of some way to stop the sailing.

Chapter Forty

SHORTLY AFTER ELEVEN there was a lot of noise and movement at the main gate. Something was happening. I watched as men milled about and opened a second gate that doubled the size of the entrance to the compound.

A low-loader edged into the compound, carrying the kind of thing that had probably never ever been inside Josh's compound before.

'It's here,' Blue said with satisfaction.

I didn't say anything at all. I just stared, astonished.

There was no doubt about what it was. Mystery over. It was a tank.

'A main battle tank,' Blue said with evident satisfaction.

'Where's it from?'

He just chuckled.

It was so shiny and new-looking that there was only one place it could have come from: the factory. The old Armstrong Works in Scotswood on Tyneside was where they were made. At least, they had been until the closure of the works a year or two earlier, as part of yet more government cost-cutting and military downsizing. This one looked as if it had been one of the last to come off the process belt.

I stared at the enormity of the thing on the truck and shook my head with awe. Senga and I hadn't come up with this when we were speculating about Blue's planned contribution to the ship's cargo.

'Where's it going?'

'You know that. Marseilles.'

'And then?'

He shook his head impatiently and walked forward to clamber up the side of the low-loader, intent on checking that the load was secure.

At present there was no space for it on the ship. I knew that without using a measuring tape.

'We'll have to offload stuff to make way for it,' I called after him.

'Get on with it, then!'

'Release the boy first.'

He turned and stared hard at me.

'Get Tom out here where I can see him, while I talk to Josh about getting stuff unloaded to make way for this thing.'

He thought for a moment and then signalled to the Land Cruiser. A door opened. Tom spilled out, propelled by whoever remained inside. He stumbled, fell, picked himself up and looked towards us. I waved him over and waited until he arrived.

'Are you all right, Tom?'

'Yeah. The bastards! They broke Julie's door down. I couldn't believe it. Julie—'

'Forget Julie for the moment, Tom. There's more important things going on here.'

He bridled at that and was about to argue.

'Shut up, Tom!'

Wisely, he shut up.

By then, two thugs had arrived to stand either side of him. A couple more were close to their vehicle. The odds were not good. I ruled out trying anything.

Blue joined us. 'He stays with me,' he said with a nod towards Tom.

'Until the cargo is aboard?'

'And afterwards. We're both going with it.'

I grimaced but it was no time to argue. I left Tom there on the jetty and went to see his father.

Josh met me as I reached the deck. 'What the hell's that thing on the jetty?'

'A main battle tank. He wants us to make space for it.'

'Where?'

'Take something off.'

'Like what?'

'Just do it, Josh. Keep him sweet.'

I didn't want a debate just then, not with Blue watching and waiting. There was no telling how he would react to us making difficulties.

It took time to arrange, but we got it done. Josh had the crew take off a combine harvester and a big excavator, and then shuffled other stuff around to make space.

The main battle tank came aboard. I watched, more determined than ever that this had to be stopped, and as uncertain as ever how to do it.

While all this was going on, Josh became a bit distracted.

'Anything wrong?' I asked.

He shook his head. 'I don't know. Anne's not answering her phone.'

'Maybe she's got nothing more to say to you?' I said with a grin.

'That's what I'm worried about. She blames me for everything. Mind you, she has good reason, I suppose.'

I patted him on the shoulder. 'Come on, Josh. She'll come round. She's probably busy right now. What was she going to do this morning anyway?'

'She said she was going to the supermarket.'

'There you are, then. She's busy.'

'Yeah. You're probably right.'

I probably was right, but I wasn't sure. When I got away from Josh I took out my phone and rang both the Steeles' house and Anne's mobile. No reply from either of them.

Nothing really to worry about, but I *was* worried. My feeling was that as an anxious mother, Anne would be desperate to take a phone call that morning. She would be hanging on, biting her lip, desperate for news. So why wasn't she there?

Blue beckoned me over when the loading was complete.

'We will sail this evening,' he said. 'Ten p.m. Tell Steele to make sure the captain has everything ready. I will return before then.'

'Not until ten tonight?'

'Just be ready!'

I shrugged. 'OK. And you're going with the ship?'

He nodded.

'And Logan?'

'Just me – and Steele's kid.'

'Anyone else? The captain will need to know.'

He shook his head. 'No one else.'

That was what he thought.

They left, taking Tom with them as their hostage. I watched them go. Then I sought out Josh again. He was in a bitter mood.

'You just let them take Tom?' he said.

'We want him back alive, Josh, not killed in a shoot-out on the dockside.'

'I suppose so,' he admitted, looking despondent. 'So what happens now?'

'Blue wants the ship to leave at ten tonight. He'll be back before then, with Tom.'

'Anyone else?'

I shook my head. 'We've got things to sort out before tonight, Josh.'

'Like what? All I'm concerned about is Tom.'

'Tom's part of it, but he's not the whole thing.'

'He is to me, and to Anne.'

'I appreciate how you both feel, but it's not only about him, is it? It never was.'

'I don't know what you mean.'

'I told you I'm not letting Logan get away with exporting a shipload of stolen goods. Now it's worse. Look down there. That's a main battle tank – not a bloody tractor!'

'That thing could do a lot of damage in the wrong hands. There's no way I'm going to allow that to end up with some guerrilla group in North Africa, which is where it's likely to be going from Marseilles.'

'I don't give a toss about any of that,' Josh said defiantly. 'I'm only interested in Tom.'

He turned and walked off to see the captain, leaving me to fret and stew. What the hell to do now?

I'd got a phone number for Logan that Josh had given me. I debated for a moment and then I rang him.

'Logan? This is Frank Doy.'

'How did you get this number?'

'From Josh Steele. He's worried. His wife isn't answering her phone. That's not anything to do with you, is it?'

He chuckled. 'His security people are crap! They might as well not have been there. Personally, I would fire the whole lot of them. Tell him that from me!'

So my hunch had been right. They must have picked her up from the shopping expedition. Easier than at the house.

I kept calm. 'What's this about? You've already got the boy.'

'It's insurance – my insurance. The boy's not with me, is he?'

No, he wasn't. It sounded like the partnership was dissolving. Now Logan and Blue each had a piece of the Steele family for bargaining purposes.

'Don't let anything happen to her,' I warned.

He chuckled again. 'Just do what we agreed, Doy.'

The phone went dead. I studied it for a moment but it

188

stayed like that. For now, I just had to hope Anne was in better shape.

A couple of minutes later I fielded a call from Bill Peart.

'What's going on?' he asked.

'Not a lot,' I lied. 'Anything happening your end?'

'It depends on how you look at it, I suppose. Remember I told you we had a badly injured cop, beaten up by some thugs associated with Logan?'

'I remember.'

'Well, he didn't make it. Died this morning. Wife and two kids there with him.'

I winced. 'I'm sorry to hear that, Bill.'

'Nothing to do with your client, of course?'

'Well ...' I blew out with frustration and anger. 'You can't tie that to me or to Josh Steele, Bill. Josh is a victim in all this, and I'm a ... I don't know what the hell I am now! A bystander, I guess.'

'Yeah, well. You've just got a remarkable talent for being in the wrong place, I suppose.'

I ignored that. But it wasn't entirely unfair.

'How's the investigation going? Any progress?'

'Not much,' he said morosely. 'But we're planning to search Steele's ship. What do you think we'll find, Frank? Anything interesting?'

That winded me for a moment.

'Frank?'

'I'm still here. Just surprised. I don't know what you'll find, Bill. I haven't a clue.'

He rang off soon afterwards, leaving me sweating blood.

I went looking for Josh again.

'It's just got worse,' I told him. 'More urgent, anyway. Cleveland police are planning on searching your ship.'

'What the hell for?'

I shrugged. 'Beats me. All I know is we have to do something. That shipment has to be stopped, but it can't just sit here for the cops to find. You and the rest of your family are likely to end up in jail if that happens. Me, too, probably.'

'There's still Tom,' he pointed out.

I nodded. There was still Tom. There was also Anne now, but I wasn't going to tell Josh that for the moment. I couldn't afford to risk him doing something else totally stupid.

A car drove onto the jetty and stopped. Senga got out and waved to us. Josh raised a hand to acknowledge her in a desultory sort of way. I just stared. Then something clicked.

'That's it!' I said breathlessly. 'Senga came up with the right idea the other night.'

Chapter Forty-One

'WHAT WAS THAT?' Josh said.

'When I was saying to her we had to find a way of getting rid of Logan and Blue permanently, Senga suggested it might be easier to make the ship disappear. I think she's right.'

'Make the bloody ship disappear? Don't talk daft! You're as loopy as she is.'

'Just think about it, Josh. We could sink the damned thing!'

He swore bitterly and turned to walk away. I grabbed his arm. 'Come and sit down with me and Senga. Hear us out.'

'Don't be so stupid!' he said angrily.

But he came with me to meet his sister-in-law. Then the three of us retired to a nearby cabin.

'What's going on?' Senga asked, sensing the atmosphere.

'He wants to sink the bloody ship,' Josh said. 'I gather you suggested that?'

'Well, not quite,' she said with a chuckle. 'Disappear it, is what I said. But sinking it will do the job. What's that big thing on deck, by the way? Is it what I think it is?'

'A main battle tank,' I said, 'as currently used by the British Army. You might well look surprised,' I added, as she raised her eyebrows and gave a little whistle.

'A tank?'

'That's the special item Blue was on about. I suspect it's why he came here in the first place.'

'A tank?' Senga said again, thoughtfully. 'We didn't think of that, did we?'

I just shook my head. I wasn't in the mood for whimsical conversation. I wanted to get down to business.

'It changes things,' I said. 'They were already pretty bad, but this makes them worse. There's no way we can let them ship out a weapon like that. God knows who the customer is but it won't be a friend of this country, or of the West. Probably some guerrilla group in North Africa, like I just said to Josh.

'Also,' I added, 'the Cleveland police are planning to search the ship. We can't let that happen either. Finally, they still have Tom. That's it, I think – all the news.'

I refrained from mentioning Anne. None of us could do anything about that for the moment. To say anything now would just clutter things up with emotion. What we needed was brainpower.

'So what are we going to do?' Senga asked.

'I like your idea,' I said. 'We'll sink the ship.'

'No, you bloody won't!' Josh said angrily. 'Tell me how that would work. Tell me how that could possibly make things better.'

'First, it would mean the tank goes nowhere. Just to the bottom of the sea. Second, if the ship is gone, there's nothing for the police to find – and nothing to incriminate you. Third, Logan won't get the rest of the shipment either. In fact, he'll get nothing at all. How am I doing so far?'

'But I'm down a ship plus a legitimate cargo,' Josh pointed out. 'And they've still got Tom.'

'True.'

There *was* that. Hell, I couldn't think of everything!

'Frank will rescue Tom,' Senga said confidently. 'The rest of it – the ship and the cargo – doesn't really matter, does it?'

They both looked at me then.

'You'll rescue Tom?' Josh said, sounding mystified.

'Yes,' I said.

'How?'

'I don't know yet. I'm still working on it.'

There followed a long pause. Then Josh sighed and said, 'OK. Let's do it.'

The preparations for departure took all day. The crew had to make sure the cargo was battened down tight, which took some doing. Then the ship itself had to be made seaworthy. Josh had to brief the captain and chief engineer, and make sure they understood what was expected of them. There were also arrangements to be made with officials of one sort or another on shore.

And I had to find somewhere to hide on the ship, because I was sailing with it.

*

Blue and a couple of armed guards turned up an hour or so before the ship was due to leave. They brought Tom with them and hustled him aboard and into a cabin that Blue locked.

Josh remonstrated with him about Tom, demanding that he let the boy go.

'He's my insurance,' Blue snapped. 'I don't want to be intercepted by anybody's navy because you've blown the whistle on us.'

Josh, visibly deflated, turned away, defeated.

'Where's Doy?' I heard Blue ask.

'No idea.'

Josh shrugged and walked away.

I had thought Senga might have turned up to check on Tom but I couldn't see her from my vantage point amongst the deck cargo. What I did see was that Blue brought only a couple of men on board with him. No doubt to share watchman duties. He wasn't going to be able to stay awake all the way to Marseilles.

We slid away from the jetty on time and headed downriver. It was a cold night, but very clear. Stars and frost, and an arctic breeze to make the eyes water. But no more snow.

I was hidden on deck, sheltered from the breeze by the cargo, and I watched the banks of the Tees slip past us. The Transporter Bridge soon receded, and then all the clutter on the river banks began to pass us by.

There was plenty for me to think about. Tom was part of it, but he was OK for the moment. I concentrated on keeping out of the way of Blue and his men, who were patrolling the ship. I had to avoid them for the next few hours, at least. Until the rendezvous. Then teamwork would kick in. Sinking a ship is a more complex project than you might think – if you want everyone on it to survive. Well, nearly everyone.

I could have made my play right away but I settled down to wait until we were well out to sea and the edge had come off Blue's vigilance. No hurry now, not when we had come this far.

The petro-chemical complex south of the river slid by, along with the Hartlepool nuclear power station and the remaining wild land around Greatham Creek and Seal Sands. The tide was running out strongly and there were mud flats and sandy beaches to either side of us, coated with rime and glistening in the moonlight.

We passed North Gare Sands and, on the southern bank of the river, the steelworks at Redcar. Soon after that we reached the entrance to the estuary and passed between the South Gare and North Gare breakwaters, and out into Tees Bay and the desolate North Sea.

The crew of the ss *Anne* numbered about half a dozen, including the skipper. That was enough. With all the technical equipment they have to aid them, a crew that size can sail the biggest cargo ships afloat these days. The small number suited me. It meant I could move about easily unnoticed, and it meant there were fewer people likely to get shot if a firefight started up.

Once we were out to sea I seemed to be the only person on deck. That was until Blue and a couple of his men came outside and stood talking. The men – Eddie and Manny, I gathered they were called – were smoking, and laughing and joking. They obviously thought it all a great wheeze. Not Blue, though. He seemed distracted, no doubt thinking about the voyage and what awaited him at the far end.

After a couple of minutes, without any warning whatsoever, Blue calmly pulled out a gun and shot the pair of them. I was shocked by the sudden, unanticipated violence. Almost before their bodies hit the deck, Blue tipped them over the side, one after the other. He didn't need them anymore, it seemed.

That was likely to be Tom's fate, too, I thought, once he was no longer needed. It was a useful, if grim, pointer to the kind of man Blue was. I would remember that when the time came.

Chapter Forty-Two

SO THERE WAS just Blue left now. That made it easier. I certainly wasn't going to underestimate him, but one man was a lot different to three. Before I went looking for him, I checked the Glock I'd brought with me. There was no way I was going up against him unarmed, especially given what I'd just seen him do.

He was on the bridge with the captain, watching him, monitoring his movements, and no doubt ready to pounce if something wasn't right. I slid away. I would tackle him, but not yet. First, I wanted to see how Tom was doing.

I referred to the place where Tom had been locked up as a cabin, but it certainly wasn't a luxury cabin. More of a steel box in which a bunk bed had been installed. There wasn't even a porthole. I wondered if it had been a punishment cell, or a holding cell for crew members guilty of serious misdemeanours. A ship has to have somewhere like that.

The door was fastened tight, secured by levers. It reminded me of a watertight bulkhead in a submarine. You didn't need a key to open it from the outside. I pocketed my gun and began to turn the levers to open the door.

'That'll do!' a voice said. I froze. Then I gently turned my head. Blue was there. He stood in the narrow passageway, gun pointed at me.

'I wondered if you might turn up,' he said. 'This makes it easy.'

I stepped back from the door. 'Just checking to see if the boy is all right.'

'Yeah? Well, you might as well open the door all the way now, and join him.'

'Then what?'

'Just open the door.'

The future was uncertain, and probably would be brief. I had a gun, and he hadn't searched me, but the gun was in my pocket. I couldn't draw it out faster than a bullet could come from his gun to me. My life was being lived a second at a time now.

He motioned to me to get on with it. I turned back to the door and worked the bottom lever. As I straightened up again, a door behind Blue opened and to my astonishment Senga stepped into the corridor. She was dressed in some sort of waitress uniform and carrying a tray of coffee mugs.

Christ, no! I gaped at her. Senga and the Frenchman? All my fears and suspicions returned in a rush.

Where the hell had she come from? Our eyes met, and mine must have betrayed my utter dejection. Hers seemed full of fury and contempt. Blue was her man, it seemed.

All those thoughts flashed through my mind in the briefest of moments. Then the cabin door swung open, giving me a brief glimpse of a startled Tom.

At the same time, Senga screamed horrendously and threw the tray against the wall with an almighty crash that reverberated excruciatingly in the confines of the narrow, steel-lined corridor.

Pandemonium broke out.

Blue swung round, gun raised, as Senga withdrew through the doorway from which she had appeared.

Like a jack-in-the-box released, Tom bolted past me into the corridor, and cannoned into Blue. With a curse, Blue grabbed him and pushed him, struggling, back towards the cell.

I shoulder-charged the pair of them. Blue tripped over the high threshold, and went down hard inside the cell. Tom leapt up and back outside again with an agility I would never have expected of him.

Unthinkingly, I slammed the door shut and spun the levers back into the lock position. Then I slumped back against the wall with relief.

'You all right, Tom?' I managed to gasp as I fought for breath.

He nodded and grinned. 'Got the bastard!'

I just shook my head, still shaking from the frenzy of the last few moments, and from the agony of my doubts about Senga.

Tom said, 'How many more of them are there onboard?'

'There's just him. He shot the rest.'

'Really?' Tom grinned and slapped the cell door hard. 'Well, we've got him now!'

I had to agree. We had him.

'He's still got his gun, though,' I pointed out.

'He'd need a bomb to get through that door, or the wall,' Tom said scornfully.

'Well done, kid!' I said belatedly, grinning and punching him lightly in the shoulder. 'You saved the day.'

'I finally did something right, eh?' he said happily.

'Something brave, too,' I told him. 'You're a bloody idiot!' I added with a chuckle.

'Oh, I wasn't thinking,' he said modestly. 'I was so mad I just went for him.'

Then the door along the passage slammed open again and Senga stuck her head round the corner.

'Where is he?' she mimed.

I just shrugged, still a bit dazed by the passage of events.

'In there!' Tom said, pointing at the locked door.

Senga whooped and threw her arms into the air in joyful celebration. I smiled. But inwardly I cringed, wondering how on earth I could have got it, and her, so wrong – even for one moment.

'You two!' I complained.

Senga gave me a big grin.

'What on earth are you doing here?' I asked her, still struggling to reconcile my conflicting emotions.

'I'm a galley cook – or whatever they're called.'

'Since when?'

'Since I discovered you were going to be aboard. You didn't think I was going to let you sail without me, did you? I knew you wouldn't be able to manage on your own.'

I shook my head, with astonishment this time, and gave her a hug. 'Your timing was perfect,' I assured her. 'I thought you and—'

'What did you think?' she demanded.

'It doesn't matter,' I said faintly, wondering again how I could have got it so wrong.

'What? Me and Blue?'

I shrugged. 'I was told you had a French boyfriend.'

'Armand is long gone,' she said. 'He was an artist anyway, not a bloody criminal!'

I just shrugged again, even more helplessly.

'I was trying to help,' she said earnestly.

'And you did!' I assured her, strength returning.

'Did I really?' she said, grinning. 'I did, didn't I?'

I nodded and hugged her hard. Then I went to see the captain.

'Everything's under control now,' I told him. 'We've got Monsieur Bleu safely locked up.'

'Phew!' He rubbed his face with both hands and then said, 'What about the others?'

'He'd already shot them and tipped them overboard. He didn't need them anymore.'

The captain blew out his cheeks with relief and shook his head. 'I don't want to know how you managed it,' he said, 'but thank God it's over! Another two hours to go,' he added. 'The rendezvous has been moved back an hour.'

'That's not a problem, is it?'

He shook his head. 'We'll just pull the plug an hour later, that's all. Ask that new galley maid if she can brew some more coffee, will you?' he added with a grin.

I helped, Tom helped, and between the three of us we managed to brew up coffee. The crew came up one at a time to grab some. Senga took a mug to the captain.

'You did really well, Tom,' I said, when we had a spare moment. 'I thought we'd had it back there.'

He gave me a big grin. 'I was desperate to get out of that claustrophobic cell. I would have charged a machinegun when the door opened!'

'Is there any way Blue can get out of there? We don't want him reappearing.'

Tom shook his head emphatically. 'I told you, it's just a steel box. That's all it is. Houdini couldn't get out. Not even a microwave can get through the walls.'

'So he can't phone for help either?'

Tom shook his head. 'It's a dead zone. There's no mobile service at all. I know. I tried.'

Just then Senga returned, looking remarkably pleased with herself.

'What are you smiling about?' Tom asked her.

'The captain asked me if I wanted a permanent job. He really likes my coffee.'

'Our coffee!' Tom reminded her. 'It wasn't just you that made it.'

She put her tongue out at him. But all was well with our little world now.

Chapter Forty-Three

IT WAS COMING up to three when the captain told me they'd got something on the radar. I stepped outside to let him get on with his job without distraction. For a couple of minutes longer I could hear nothing except the swish of the ship easing through the sea. Then I picked up a distant sound as it came in fast, lights blazing.

It was a big one, a Chinook. I watched it hover and then begin to descend towards a landing pad on the upper deck. The noise by then was deafening, and it didn't stop when the chopper touched down. The rotor blades kept whirling. It was to be a short stay.

I saw Josh climb in through the open doorway and disappear for a moment. Then he reappeared and beckoned. Members of the crew dropped what they were doing and headed for the chopper. I steered Senga and Tom the same way, telling them I would join them in a couple of minutes.

'Where are you going?' Senga demanded.

'I'm going to get Blue.'

She wanted to argue but I had no time for that. I turned away and headed back down to the place where we'd left him.

The ship had lost its way now, and its movement had changed. There was a perceptible difference, an uneasy wallowing that was disconcerting as I crossed the deck and went down a flight of steps. It felt like the end was coming.

I hesitated outside the cabin. I really didn't want to do this. I wanted to be safe on the chopper with the others. But there was no way I could just leave the guy, trapped and soon to drown, much though part of me wanted to do just that.

One problem I had to face was his gun. Another was time. There was very little of it for discussion, still less for negotiation. It was now or never. Time was nearly up.

I rapped on the door with my own gun to warn him and began to spin the levers that would open it. When the door was free, I stood to one side and opened it a couple of inches. Then I called to him unseen and made my pitch.

'Blue, stay where you are for the moment, but we need to talk. And you've got a decision to take.'

'Is that right?'

He sounded calm, in control of himself. I was relieved. Perhaps we could talk sensibly.

'The ship is sinking.'

'Crap!'

'We've pulled the plug. We're scuttling it, and a helicopter will take us all off in the next few minutes. If you want to come with us, you're going to have to accept my terms for letting you out of there.'

'Or what?'

'Or I shut the door again and you can stay where you are. It's up to you.'

Tense, I waited for ... what? Bullets? A charge at the door?

'OK,' he said. 'Go on. What are you offering?'

I breathed more easily. He was listening. He was being reasonable.

'If you come with us, you'll be under armed guard and you'll be handed over to the police when we get back to Middlesbrough. Then it will be up to them. OK?'

He hesitated, weighing it up. Then he said, 'How would we do it?'

'First, I want you to slide your gun across the floor, so I can see it. Then I want you to sit on the floor well away from the gun. When I'm satisfied you've done that, I'll open the door wider and bring you out. OK?'

I waited until a gun appeared on the floor, without a hand holding it. Then I paused a moment to rub my brow with the back of my hand. The next bit was going to be tricky.

'You're sitting down?'

'Yeah.'

I edged the door open a little more and risked a quick glance round the edge. He was sitting down on the floor on the far side of the cabin. I blew out with relief and opened the door wider, ready to take the next step.

'What now?' he said.

'Stay where you are,' I told him.

I edged into the cell, covering him with the Glock. He didn't move. I kept going until I stood next to the gun he'd slid along the floor. Then I reached down and picked it up, without letting my eyes leave him.

'The ship's going down, eh?' he said conversationally.

'Yeah. Together with the Challenger tank and all that stuff

Logan stole, plus Steele's legal cargo. The whole damned lot's going down. It's the only way. Logan's going to be pissed.'

'Logan,' he said with a wry smile.

I motioned to him to get to his feet and lean against a wall. Then I patted him down, searching for another weapon.

'He's not your boss, is he?' I said.

'Logan?'

'Yeah.'

Still smiling, he shook his head.

But something was wrong here, I realized. For a guy in his position, he was far too relaxed and comfortable. I couldn't see why.

'If the ship's going down,' he said quietly, giving me another little smile, 'we'd better get out of here.'

There it was again, that expression of quiet confidence in himself. He behaved as if he was the one in control. I couldn't understand it. But he was right. We had to move.

'I want to propose a deal,' he said quietly.

'I thought we had one?' I stared hard at him, wondering where he was going with this.

He shook his head. 'Not one I can live with.'

'Then what?' I asked, perplexed. 'You'd rather stay here?'

Again he shook his head. 'I'm not going with you. It's as simple as that. I want you to cut me loose in a lifeboat. Do that, and I'll be in your debt. You can name your price.'

I just stared at him.

Chapter Forty-Four

THE INITIAL URGE to give him an angry mouthful passed. Was he serious? I realized he was.

'Which part don't you fancy,' I asked him, 'Middlesbrough or police custody?'

He just smiled.

Keeping well away from him, I thought fast. Could I trust him? No. Should I listen to him? Maybe. Why not?

The ship gave some alarming creaks that vibrated along the length of the wall nearest to us. I managed not to flinch, but it was worrying.

Blue looked around with interest. 'We haven't got much time,' he pointed out, 'if what you say is true.'

'Oh, it's true, right enough. I'm just considering what you said.'

'Better be quick.'

Amazingly, he seemed more relaxed than I was. I had to hand it to him.

'What can I help you with?' he asked conversationally. 'There must be something you need, or want.'

There certainly was, but ... I laughed in his face. 'There are a couple of things I want,' I told him, 'but you can't help with either of them.'

'Try me. Is one of them to do with the boy?'

Astute bugger!

I nodded. 'The boy, yes. I would consider doing a deal with you if you could guarantee that the boy will be safe, now and in the future.'

'OK. What about his old man? Do you want security for him, too?'

The ship lurched, and a whole series of vibrations ran through the deck beneath our feet. It was going down, and fast.

I smiled ruefully. 'Come on,' I said. 'We're wasting valuable time. Let's get out of here.'

He stayed right where he was. 'I can deliver security for them both,' he said, 'now and in the future – permanently.'

I stared at him. 'And how can you do that?'

He shook his head impatiently and said, 'Is there anything else?'

'You've taken his mother hostage. I want her released.'

'His mother?' His eyebrows shot up and he shook his head. 'I know nothing about that. It must be Logan's doing. But I can fix that as well.'

'How?' I said again.

'Let me make a couple of phone calls.'

I hesitated. What was he up to?

'You have nothing to lose,' he pointed out calmly.

No? Perhaps not.

There was nothing he could do to turn the situation round, so far as I could see. He couldn't organize a rescue party out here. There was no time. A reception party back on land was out of the question, as well. Armed cops would be waiting for us when we landed.

'No tricks, I promise you,' he said briskly. 'This is a straightforward deal between me and you. Whatever happened in the past, it's over. It was never personal anyway. I hold nothing against you.'

Curiously, perhaps, I understood and accepted that. I knew what he meant. For him, it was strictly business, and had been since the outset. Nothing personal, as he said. The unfortunate Bryce Logan had not been his son, after all.

What was in it for him now? Well, that was no mystery. He wanted his freedom, even if it was on the open seas. He would take his chances. That was better than the certain prospect of the rest of his life in prison.

For me, if there was a chance of getting Tom Steele out of the hole he and his family had dug, it was a chance worth taking. But could it be done? It seemed unlikely.

Yet what would change if Blue didn't, or couldn't, deliver? Nothing. Absolutely nothing. Tom would be no worse off.

The ship suddenly lurched and it seemed as if there would be no end to the creaks and vibrations this time. We were going down.

'One call,' I snapped. 'Make it fast.'

He shook his head. 'Two,' he said firmly. 'Two, and they must be private.'

I shrugged and walked away a few paces. 'OK,' I said, turning back towards him. 'Come out of there and make your calls.'

Senga appeared on the ladder in the companionway.

'What's going on?' she mouthed.

I gave her a thumbs-up and a smile.

She looked anxious, not surprisingly. But she seemed prepared to wait.

Blue walked towards me a minute or two later. 'It's done,' he said.

I waited.

'Tomorrow – today, I should say – at ten a.m. exactly, you and the woman—' He broke off to nod towards Senga, 'You must visit Logan in the farmhouse where he is staying. Do you know where that is?'

'Near Greatham?'

'That's right. You must go there. Nobody else. Just the two of you.'

'What happens then?'

'You will receive proof that I am keeping my side of the bargain. Now, if you would be so good, I would appreciate your help in launching a lifeboat.'

I stared at him, thinking, calculating. What proof did I have, here and now, that what he had promised would happen? None, none at all.

'You are wondering if you can trust me?' he said mildly.

I nodded. 'Of course.'

'You have my word.'

'Not good enough,' I said.

Astonishingly, he seemed surprised. 'Where I come from...' he began. Then he stopped and shrugged.

'OK. These modern lifeboats all have homing devices,' he said. 'If this morning you do not receive the guarantee that you require, then feel free to alert the authorities to search for me.'

He wouldn't have got far by then. They would find him pretty quickly.

'Frank!' Senga called anxiously. 'We have to go.'

'In a moment,' I called back.

'Now, Frank! The pilot says now.'

Blue resumed, undistracted.

'If you or the authorities visit the farmhouse before ten a.m.,' he said calmly, 'you will not receive the guarantee you require. I repeat: you and the woman, and nobody else, must go there at the time I have said. If you are not satisfied, advise the authorities to arrest Logan and to look for me. It is that simple,' he concluded.

Simple? It wasn't. Of course it wasn't.

'As for now,' he added with a dismissive gesture, 'I will not go with you. So you must decide soon, I think, or it will be too late for us all.'

I did the algorithm. It was brutal. If we took Blue with us, there would be no guarantees for the future of the Steele family. Simple as that. Blue would be arrested, charged, and imprisoned probably, and so would Logan be, but the Steeles would continue to live in fear and jeopardy.

In any case, how could I get him aboard the chopper now if he refused to go? I believed him implicitly when he said he wouldn't leave with us. And leave soon was what we had to do.

'Frank!' Senga called again.

She was beginning to sound fearful. It wasn't surprising. The ship was making unnatural sounds and movements, and there were more and more of them. The ss *Anne* was screaming to be put out of her misery.

I decided it was worth a shot. If nothing came of it, the cops could collect Logan and gang, and probably find Blue as well. He wouldn't have got far in a lifeboat in just a few hours.

'OK,' I told him. 'Let's do it.'

Chapter Forty-Five

WITH THE AID of a couple of crew members, we got it done. The lifeboat dropped into the sea, with Blue in it. Then we scrambled into the chopper. The captain was there, along with the rest of his crew. Tom was there. So was Josh. Josh was talking to the pilot, and no doubt urging patience and understanding.

One or two of the men grinned at me and made hand signals

to suggest I had been holding things up. Fortunately, it was too noisy to ask or answer questions. We sat down on long bench seats, as if we were paratroopers. Someone slammed the door shut and moments later the Chinook lifted off.

Senga stared at me, desperate for an explanation. 'Not now,' I told her, pointing to my ear. 'I'm a bit deaf. I'll tell you later.'

She seemed ready to argue the point but then she gave up and settled back, leaving me to consider how much I would tell her anyway.

We didn't fly away speedily. Not immediately. We hovered for a few minutes and we circled. Josh gestured for me to come to a window beside him. I moved over. Then I stood with him, and together we watched waves begin to break over the SS *Anne* as she settled in the water.

The pilot took us in gentle circles for a few minutes, and we watched until the sea came up and over the bridge of the ship. In all the turmoil, I didn't even notice the lifeboat. In fact, I forgot to look for it. Josh looked at me with a question in his eyes and on his lips: *Enough?*

I nodded. It was enough. I turned away to sit back down next to Senga. She smiled and took my arm. Conversation was virtually impossible, given the noise level, but conversation wasn't needed. Certainly not by me.

The captain glanced across from where he sat and gave me a wry smile. I nodded back. It was probably a sad moment for him, but he was taking it very well. At least he didn't have to go down with his ship.

Josh went forward to speak to the pilot again. The engine noise increased. I felt the power surge through the Chinook as it began the homeward flight. A last glance over my shoulder revealed no sign now of the SS *Anne*. It was as if she had never been. I couldn't say that about Blue.

Back at Josh's compound, there was a holiday atmosphere. Josh and Tom were laughing and punching each other. Julie was there, talking wildly to Senga. Gerald was there, too, organizing drinks and food for everyone. I wondered if the man ever went home. I also wondered what price he would get for his memoirs, if he ever chose to write them.

Only Anne wasn't there, and nobody was talking about that for the moment. It was the middle of the night. Perhaps they thought she was home, in bed. I didn't ask.

No one seemed interested in the man we had left in the lifeboat either, or indeed in the two men he had shot and tipped overboard. Not to mention all the others no doubt down to him in a long criminal career of abductions, murders and whatever else he had been up to. Still, he was a man alone in perilous circumstances. I couldn't forget that.

'What are you thinking about?' Senga asked, joining me and linking her arm in mine.

'Blue.'

'What? Out there, all alone?'

I nodded, surprised she had picked up on that thought.

'And that worries you?'

'It concerns me.'

That was only part of it, of course, a small part. I was also wondering what he was going to do. Did he have anything in mind? Or was evading the police and arrest enough for him? Perhaps being in control of his own destiny still was all that really mattered. He was a tough guy. I wouldn't say I admired him, but he was impressive.

'Tell me, Frank, what would have happened if he'd overpowered you when you opened the door?'

I sighed. 'He would have shot me, and whoever else got in his way. I don't have any doubts about that whatsoever.'

I grinned and added, 'He would have taken the helicopter, as well, and tipped you lot out!'

'There you are, then. You did the right thing. He'd caused enough trouble in his life.'

'What a sensible woman you are!'

Senga obviously thought his life was as good as over now. I wasn't so sure.

I held off for the moment from telling her that we both had a continuing role to play. There would be time for that soon enough.

'Frank,' she added solemnly. 'Back there ... you know, back when ... you didn't really distrust me, did you?'

'Of course not,' I lied.

She smiled and said, 'Come and join the party.'

Josh was in good form. After a little while he took me aside and we planted ourselves on easy chairs in his office, nursing mugs of coffee from a fancy machine that made every kind of coffee known to man, and then some.

'What do you think?' Josh asked happily.

I smiled. 'Well, we've certainly solved a couple of problems, Josh. We've got Tom back, and the police won't be able to find anything incriminating on the ship now.'

He chuckled. 'That was a brilliant idea of Senga's.'

I thought so too.

But there was still a lot of sorting out to do. We had trumped the police search and stopped delivery of the tank, but Anne was missing and so far as I knew the threat to Tom remained in place. The police wouldn't have given up either. We weren't out of the woods yet. We had scarcely reached the woodland edge.

Josh looked at me with a funny expression on his face and said, 'Are you and her...?'

'Me and Senga? Oh, I don't know, Josh. Let's just wait and see, shall we?'

'Of course,' he said, grinning. 'Good luck with that!'

I stirred my coffee with a plastic spoon, chasing bubbles around the surface. I was hoping the exercise would help me think more clearly. Josh didn't seem to know that his wife was missing, abducted. What would be gained by me telling him?

I decided it could wait a few more hours. I didn't want him running around in circles tearing his hair out. Nor did I want to rain on his parade. Not just yet anyway. That could wait till ten o'clock. Meanwhile, let him exult in the safe return of his son.

'Of course,' he reflected soberly, 'I've lost all that merchandise.'

'And a ship.'

'At least some good will come of that, though,' he said with a grin.

'Oh?'

'The ss *Anne* will be a natural sea park in a few years' time, a man-made reef – a divers' paradise! It will teem with wildlife.'

'Just like Middlesbrough.'

'In the old days,' he agreed with a chuckle.

'By the way,' I added, 'I was surprised your skipper wasn't more upset about losing his ship.'

Josh laughed. 'You know why?'

'It wouldn't be anything to do with money, would it?'

'What a cynic you are, Frank! Why, no. It wasn't that at all.'

'What, then?'

'He's getting a new ship out of it. I promised him a bigger and better one, once the insurance comes through.'

'And you call me cynical?'

Senga had to be told what lay ahead, of course. It wasn't very far ahead either. I glanced at my watch when I got away from Josh. Eight now. Whether it proved to be a waste of time or not, we had to be at the farmhouse in the Greatham marshes at ten. Just the two of us. No one else.

Chapter Forty-Six

THE OLD FARMHOUSE was set on a small hillock that put it just above the traditional flood level in the marshes. A few stunted trees, hawthorn, Scots pine and sycamore, did little to provide shelter in such a bleak place. The house looked cold and damp as we approached it along the deeply rutted track that once had been a tarmac drive but now had turned to gravel and pools of water. It was a house fit for someone who didn't care much for neighbours, someone who valued privacy or had things to hide. An excellent hideout.

'It looks utterly miserable,' Senga said with a shiver.

I nodded and concentrated on avoiding the bigger potholes. That in itself was a challenge. The track was worse than the one to my house.

'There seems to be nobody about,' Senga added.

She was right. So far, there wasn't a soul in sight. What did that mean? Logan and crew had scarpered? Or were they lying in wait? We'd soon find out.

If it all went pear-shaped, as I thought likely, and if we didn't emerge alive, a sealed letter giving an account of things would find its way from my solicitor to Bill Peart.

I had wondered whether to involve Senga but in the end I felt I had no choice. Given Blue's instructions, I had to proceed as directed for there to be any chance at all of getting anything out of the deal we had agreed.

'Do you think Anne is here?' Senga asked, sounding every bit as worried as she had every right to be.

'We'll soon find out.'

As soon as I had told her about the deal with Blue there had no longer been any question of whether Senga would come with me. I couldn't have stopped her, once she knew what I had agreed. I was still worried about her, but I was much more worried about Anne. Would she be here – and alive?

I was working very hard to suppress a growing suspicion that we were on a pretty forlorn trip.

'I wonder if there'll be anyone at all here,' Senga murmured.

I shrugged. We were past the point where I had any interest in idle speculation.

'What if there isn't? What will we do then, Frank?'

'Turn loose the dogs of war!' I told her gruffly.

She laughed nervously. 'Next stop Marseilles, then?'

There were two cars parked on the far side of the farmhouse. So somebody was here. I drew up alongside the black Audi I had seen before. Senga and I looked at each other. I looked at my watch. We were in good time. Three minutes to go.

'Ready?' I asked.

She nodded.

'You can stay here, if you prefer?'

'Both of us have to be here. That was the agreement. Remember?'

'Come on, then!' I said with a forced smile. 'Let's see who's here.'

We got out of the car and turned to head for the front door, which was already open. Perhaps somebody expected us. I hoped so. But who?

As we passed by, I touched the bonnet of each car in turn. The Audi was cold. The BMW was not. Whose was that? I wondered. Who was the recent arrival?

I must have frowned then, pondering the question.

'What?' Senga whispered, staring at me intently.

I just shrugged. It was impossible to know what to expect. I should have pressed Blue harder about that when I'd had the chance.

We paused in the hall, Senga taking her cue from me. The house was still. Yet it was full of noise, myriad separate strands of sound that needed disentangling before sense could be made of them. I looked at Senga and laid a finger across my lips. She nodded.

She looked nervous, I thought, which made me wonder how I looked myself. Probably no different. No better, anyway. That was for sure.

I stood for a few moments, head down, listening hard. Somewhere nearby a fridge hummed. A wall clock in the hall measured out the passage of the seconds in funereal style. A tap dripped somewhere. A water pipe clanked. The air felt dank and chilly, but a boiler suddenly burst into life and started pulsing heat around the building.

I frowned. I could hear everything – and nothing. The house could have been empty of human occupants. And probably was. I glanced questioningly at Senga. She pulled a face and shrugged. Nothing had reached her ears either.

I moved silently across the stone floor and glanced through the open doors leading off the hall. One led to the kitchen, another to a dining room, and a third to a sitting room. They were all empty.

'I wonder where everybody is?' Senga said, breaking the silence.

I almost rebuked her for that. Just in time, I stifled my irritation, telling myself there was no need at all to maintain our silence now. There was no one here.

'Maybe they've gone for a walk?' she suggested.

'That you, Doy?' a voice called then from behind yet another door.

I started and looked at Senga, who was frozen.

'Logan?'

'In here!'

I motioned to Senga to get behind me. Then, wondering what was to come, I pushed wider the half-open door that led into a room I had not yet seen. It was an office, a sort of office at least.

The room housed a meeting table, bookshelves and an old-style partner desk, like you might see in an old-fashioned solicitor's workspace. Behind the desk was a great heavy wooden chair, oak probably, and Logan.

'Thank God!' he said.

I stared. Behind me, Senga gasped.

'How long have you been like this?' I asked.

'A long time.'

'Nobody else here?'

He didn't reply. I didn't bother asking who had tied him to the chair like this. It didn't matter. I didn't have any doubts about who was ultimately responsible.

How was this supposed to help, though? I did wonder that as I stepped forward, thinking to release him.

He shook his head. 'Sit down!'

'Frank!' Senga hissed. 'He's got a gun.'

I spun round, realizing then that there was someone else

in the room. A figure moved in the extremity of my vision. It waved a gun at me.

'Just sit down,' Logan said wearily.

There was a gun in my belt but I wasn't about to go for it. By now, it was too late for that. I sat next to Senga on chairs at the far side of the room. The figure stepped out of the shadows, but the bright light from the window behind it made all but the gun outstretched in one hand hard to see.

Things happened too fast then for me to make much sense of them. There was no time for that at all. There were sudden flashes and a couple of dull thuds. Logan slumped in his chair. Senga gave a subdued yelp. I sat still.

The figure, a man, I could see now, stooped to shoot Logan in the head again, at point-blank range. Then he straightened up and without looking at us walked out of the room.

It was only after he had gone that I realized I had no idea at all what he looked like. All I knew was that it had been a man.

Senga got to her feet, ready to follow him. I caught tight hold of her arm and shook my head. 'No!' I said urgently. 'Stay here.'

She stared at me for a moment, and then nodded. She knew. She understood. One dead was better than three.

I got up and crouched to check on Logan. But there was no need to check for a pulse, none at all.

It had been done well, I had to admit. The hit had been made with clinical speed and accuracy. Whoever the guy was, he was out of the top drawer. Minimum fuss; maximum effectiveness.

I straightened up again and turned to Senga, who was wide-eyed and shaking with delayed shock now.

'What happened?' she whispered.

I shrugged. 'What can I say? He's dead, that's all. I'd better call the police.'

'But what...? Who...?'

I took her by the hand and led her out of the room, out into the fresh marsh air. A squall was in the making. There was drizzle in the air already, and it felt good to be in it.

The BMW was gone. I hadn't even heard it.

'Let's just rest a moment,' I suggested. 'And for crissake don't ask me again what happened! I don't know.'

But I did. That had been a bit more Blue theatre, a vivid demonstration of how he had kept his side of the bargain and given me the guarantee I wanted. The Steeles would be all right now.

The demonstration, the proof, had not been without cost, though. I felt physically and psychologically drained. I had to force myself to pull out my phone and make the call that would bring Bill Peart running.

'Who was he?' Senga asked as we stood waiting.

I just shrugged. 'Don't ask me. I don't know. Anyway, it's better not to know.'

'But you do know?'

I shook my head. 'I didn't even see him, not properly.'

'But you know what happened, don't you?'

'Yes,' I admitted.

Senga, beginning to recover now, said, 'It was Blue, wasn't it? Not him personally, but ...'

I shrugged again, but I wasn't in any doubt at all. He had kept his word, mafia style. I just hadn't anticipated that.

Proof that the experience had been draining came with the realisation that I hadn't even thought of Anne for the past few minutes. Nor had Senga.

We found her, unharmed but furious, in a locked cellar. I left it to Senga to bring her up to date once I had assured her that Tom was safe too.

Chapter Forty-Seven

BILL PEART CAME to see me a day or two later, when the multi-pronged investigation was well under way. It was a big one. Apart from Logan's murder, there were other deaths and 'missing persons' to pursue. A number of Logan's men had been picked up here and there, and the forensic and pathology people were having a field day.

'It will keep us going a long time,' Bill announced with satisfaction. 'I can't even begin to estimate how much crime this investigation will solve.

'It's a great pity Logan himself died, though,' he added, giving me one of his long, thoughtful glances. 'It would have been very useful to have been able to interrogate him.'

'I'm sure it would,' I could only agree.

'A great pity Steele's ship sank, as well,' he added.

I nodded.

'And all that cargo.'

'Yes.' I shrugged. 'Josh lost his ship and its cargo. I hope the insurance helps him to recover financially.'

Bill pursed his lips but didn't disagree in actual words. 'What do you think happened?'

'To the ship? It was just one of those freak waves, apparently. I'm no deep-sea mariner myself, but I know you do get them from time to time. And that kind of ship isn't too stable at the best of times. They always look top-heavy to me.'

'Especially with a main battle tank on top of everything else?' Bill suggested.

I gritted my teeth for a moment, and then gave a judicious nod. 'There is that,' I admitted. 'Josh told you about the tank, did he?'

'He did. Wanted us to understand it was nothing to do with him. That guy called Blue had forced him to take it on board, apparently.'

'Oh?'

I was running out of things to say to Bill without exhausting my credibility with him.

'Where did the tank come from?' I asked him. 'Do you know?'

'From the tank factory on Tyneside, I'm given to understand. The old Armstrong works at Scotswood. It was a Challenger Mark II, apparently.'

'And what? They bought it? Stole it?'

'The works closed some time ago. But there were still one or two tanks being finished off or repaired there. Blue – or Monsieur Bleu, perhaps I should call him – paid someone to look the other way while one was slipped out on a low-loader.'

'Do you know where it was going?'

'It's only a guess, but it's an educated one, given the Marseilles connection. I'd say it was headed for North Africa. Libya maybe, or one of them countries in the middle of the Sahara. Imagine what folk there would have thought when a dirty great Challenger came over the dunes at them!'

'They'd probably think General Patton had returned,' I said with a grin.

I wasn't sure at that stage if Josh was going to be able to avoid all charges. It depended on what the investigation drew out. However, I thought there was a good chance that he could claim that any offences he had committed were made under duress. In fact, without the ship and without either Logan or Blue, I couldn't see how Josh could be found guilty of anything at all.

That was how it turned out. Once the abduction of both Tom and his mother had been confirmed from various sources, the police were satisfied that Josh had been under intolerable pressure and came to regard him as no more than a helpful witness against Logan and his gang. Josh could return to being a businessman and upright citizen, a pillar of the community. Why not? That seemed entirely reasonable to me.

That line of thought induced me to give Jac Picknett another phone call.

'Yes, thanks,' she said. 'Quite well. You? Good.'

How formal we were!

'Listen, Jac. Do you recall telling me about Senga giving away her baby because she couldn't look after it at the time?'

'Vaguely. Did I really tell you that?'

'You did. I was wondering what happened to the child. Do you know?'

After a bit of hesitation, Jac said, 'Well, yes. I do actually. Are you sure you want to know?'

'I am, yes. It might affect something I'm in the middle of right now.'

'Oh? How mysterious! Work or ... pleasure? No, don't tell me. I don't want to know.'

Once she had told me, it all made sense. Well, a lot of things did. I just wished I had thought to ask her earlier.

Later, much later, when Bill Peart and I took Jimmy Mack's boat out for a day's fruitless winter fishing, Bill said to me, 'I don't suppose you can cast any light on what happened to that guy Blue? Steele said the last he heard, Blue was going aboard the ss *Anne*.'

'He went down with the ship, I believe.'

Bill nodded thoughtfully. 'I thought as much.'

I wrestled with rod and line for a few moments as a

distraction, but if ever there had been anything on my hook it must have got clean away.

'Lost it, eh?' Bill said sympathetically.

I nodded.

'Can I assume,' he said heavily, after a bit of a hiatus in the conversation, 'that sometimes – just occasionally, I mean – you do tell me the truth? All of it, I mean?'

I looked at him and raised my eyebrows in surprise. 'All of it?'

He shook his head. 'No, on second thoughts, don't bother answering. I don't want to know any more.'

'Oh, look!' he added, with no suggestion of even the slightest bend in his rod, 'I've got one now.'

Later still, he added, 'The coastguard recovered a lifeboat from the ss *Anne.*'

'Really? Anybody in it?'

'Not when they found it. Makes you wonder, though, doesn't it?'

It certainly did.

I was thinking: one phone call to arrange the hit on Logan. What was the other one for – to arrange to be picked up? Probably. I didn't suppose for one moment that Blue had decided to swim ashore.

It was a pity in one way. Still, the deal had been good for both sides. The Steele family had done well out of it, and so far as I was concerned that was a worthwhile result. I would leave Bill to consider the legal ramifications, if any, and somebody else again to contemplate the moral equation.

Anne said, 'Thank you for everything you've done for us, Frank.'

'It wasn't much. All in all, it was a bit of a shambles really.'

'That's not how Josh and I see it.' She shook her head firmly. 'We couldn't have managed without you. I don't know what would have happened to Tom if you hadn't been around.'

'Tom would have coped fine, Anne. He's put up with everything thrown at him this past year and more.'

'We haven't helped much, have we?' she asked, biting her lip, tears not far away.

'You've stuck together, Anne, through the difficulties. That's the main thing. Tom wouldn't have managed without that.'

She gave a brave little smile then. 'You say the nicest things, Frank.'

'Only when they're true.'

She reached up to give me a peck on the cheek. 'Look after my sister, Frank.'

'That's all very well,' I said, 'but who's going to look after me?'

She laughed and went to join Josh, Tom and Julie in their car. Josh tooted the horn as they left. I raised a hand and waved.

Senga had come out of the house when she realized the others were leaving. 'There's just us now,' she said when she had stopped waving.

'Just us,' I agreed. 'But now you know Tom is safe. That should make a difference.'

She nodded. 'That's very important to me,' she admitted. 'More than I can say.'

'I know that now,' I told her. 'I wasn't sure for a long time, but I am now.'

'Did somebody tell you?'

'It doesn't matter, does it?' I said with a smile.

'Not really, no.'

Nothing more on the subject was said. There was no point.

But Senga knew that I understood why she would have followed Tom to the ends of the earth if he needed help. And I knew she was right to leave her son undisturbed with Anne and Josh. It was too late now to do anything else. Besides, he was in good hands.

We were quiet for a few moments. Then I took her in my arms and asked, 'Will you still stay, now things have quietened down?'

'For a little while,' she said, holding on to me tightly.

'Good.'

'Is anything else going to happen, do you think?'

'Not immediately, but something dangerous always turns up eventually.'

'Oh, good!' she said.

We looked at each other and began to laugh.